CW00642853

John Creasey – Master Storyt<

Born in Surrey, England in 1908 ...... a poor family in which
there were nine children, John Creasey grew up to be a true
master story teller and international sensation. Writing under
multiple pseudonyms, his more than 600 crime, mystery and
thriller titles have now sold 80 million copies in 25 languages.
These include many popular series such as *Gideon of Scotland
Yard, The Toff, Dr Palfrey and The Baron.*

Never one to sit still, Creasey had a strong social conscience,
and stood for Parliament several times, along with founding
the One Party Alliance which promoted the idea of government
by a coalition of the best minds from across the political
spectrum..

He also founded the Crime Writers' Association, which to this
day celebrates outstanding crime writing. The Mystery Writers
of America bestowed upon him the Edgar Award for best novel
and then in 1969 the ultimate Grand Master Award. John
Creasey's stories are as compelling today as ever.

A Backwards Jump

(Gideon's Month)

John Creasey

(writing as JJ Marric)

HOUSE OF
STRATUS

This edition published in 2012 by House of Stratus, an imprint of Stratus Books Ltd., Lisandra House, Fore Street, Looe, Cornwall, PL13 1AD, U.K.

www.houseofstratus.com

Typeset by House of Stratus.

A catalogue record for this book is available from the British Library and the Library of Congress.

ISBN 07551 - 2573-8
EAN 978 - 07551 - 2573-9

THE FIRST OF THE MONTH

I*T* was the first day of May, a beautiful day, and George Gideon was taking one of his favourite walks, through Hyde Park and across the fields. Some sheep were grazing not far off, a horde of Londoners sprawled on the grass and on chairs near the road, several riders, mostly young, trotted their horses along Rotten Row. A few people promenaded in their best clothes, as if determined to remember that this had once been London's finest fashion parade on any Sunday morning. The sunlight shimmered on the many-coloured cellulose of the rivers of cars moving in each direction, and coming slowly to a standstill whenever the police or traffic fights held them up at one of the gates.

It was half-past twelve.

Gideon had just come from Scotland Yard, where he had been since nine o'clock, working on some jobs which had needed special attention. Now he was as nearly off duty as he could ever be, content in the sun which wasn't too hot, enjoying the springiness of the grass beneath his feet, and looking forward to meeting his wife and taking her out to lunch. It was one of those rare Sundays when all five of the Gideon children still living at home were following their own devices. When Gideon had telephoned and discovered that Kate was alone, he had said: "Have a day off cooking, Kate, and come and meet me in town. I needn't stay in the office much after twelve."

She had hesitated.

"It sounds lovely, dear, but if I don't cook the joint today there'll be no cold meat for supper, or—"

"We'll eat bread and cheese, or fish and chips. How about Marble Arch at one o'clock?"

Kate had laughed.

"All right, George, I'll be there."

Kate, the dependable, would be. Gideon had decided where to take her for lunch, and he knew that she would first protest against extravagance, then thoroughly enjoy herself. Gideon was gradually developing a mood in which the occasional extravagance was both possible and wise. Two of his daughters were earning enough to keep themselves, two of the boys, too; if a twenty-five-year-old son could be called a boy. Pension days were a long way off, but at least when he retired, at sixty say, the pension and his insurances would enable him and Kate to live comfortably, and he had managed to save a bit, in spite of the long family.

The mood of contentment, like the mood of extravagance, was comparatively new to Gideon, and was partly due to achievement. It was a good thing, at fifty-one, to realise that he was practically at the top of the tree. There was just one step higher than being Commander of the Criminal Investigation Department at Scotland Yard, and that was being its Assistant Commissioner. At one time he had worried about whether he would get that plum, ever, but now he seldom gave it a thought. Whether it came or not, he couldn't complain.

He was aware, as always, of the number of people who glanced at him, some recognising, some half-recognising him. He knew, too, that even strangers looked twice, for he was big physically, with broad, heavy shoulders and a thick torso, although he wasn't actually fat. Massive was the word most often applied to Gideon. He didn't wear a hat, and his grey hair, thick and bushy, looked greyer than it was because of the sun.

He wore a suit of brown tweed which fitted loosely, and the air of well-being was with him as he took long, unhurried strides through the London which was both home and life to him. No man living knew more about its seamy side, few knew more about its warmth and tranquillity. Here was Hyde Park on a golden Sunday, looking as it always had and always would – London's favourite playground.

His mind was not on crime or criminals, and he gave none a second thought, but many a fleeting one. Across Park Lane, for instance, at one of the luxury hotels, two C.I.D. men were posing as guests and keeping an eye on a smart gentleman from Scandinavia who was probably going to try to sell property he didn't own. In the same hotel was a man who had come out of prison six months ago, after a twelve-year sentence, with full remission. So far, he was doing all right, but working as a kitchen-hand could not be expected to keep an astute mind busy, and he would brood over his wife, who had gone off with another man within a few weeks of his sentence, and also brood over his past. There wasn't much one could do for chaps like that, except have a word with them now and again, or see that someone else did, trying to make them realise that they weren't entirely alone, and outcasts.

Just along a street leading off Park Lane was the house which, two weeks ago, had been besieged by sightseers and gawpers; the house where Lucy Love had been murdered. A pretty kid, she'd had everything, or nearly everything; films, television, a career in Hollywood if she'd wanted it. She had decided to play one man off against another. Who should one be sorry for? The dead girl or her murderer, who had tried to kill himself, failed, and was now in hospital, ready to be charged the moment he came out; without any hope left.

A Rolls-Royce went by, and inside was a leading Queen's Counsel, with an income of £50,000 a year. Not long afterwards an old-fashioned but spotless black Daimler passed, driven by one of Her Majesty's judges whose salary was not much more than a tenth of the Q.C.'s. A man walking by the side of a

3

woman with three young children trailing behind straightened up abruptly when he saw Gideon: this was Sergeant Wylie, of the uniformed branch.

"Good morning, sir."

"'Morning, Sam. Lovely day. 'Morning, Mrs. Wylie." Gideon raised a hand and smiled at the children, and went on.

Earlier, he had seen another man with his wife and three children who had turned round quickly to avoid the need for speaking to Gideon; a pickpocket who would almost certainly be back in jail before the year was out. He seemed to stay out of jail just long enough to put his wife with child again, and then get sent down until the child was born. And his children were taught to steal; to pick pockets, snatch handbags, become expert in shop-lifting.

All his life Gideon had been trying to understand why a man who knew that crime didn't pay could train his children into his own anti-social folly. What would be the result if all criminal parents were separated from their children? The first thing would be an uproar about the freedom of the individual, of course, and a lot of sentimental bosh.

Gideon looked ahead at the crowds near Marble Arch, with his lips more relaxed and his eyes amused. He could hear a high-pitched voice carried to him on the quiet wind, but could not yet distinguish the words. The voice was unmistakable; he had heard it, on and off, for twenty-five years. This was Little Willie, on his Topic For the Day. It might be anything from World Government to the price of cabbages; whatever it was, he would have the biggest crowd of all the soap-box orators of the park, because he could be funny – not always intentionally. Several other speakers were up, of course, and the sun had brought them audiences much larger than usual. They were battling one against the other, gesticulating, remonstrating, condemning, threatening with hell-fire, cursing the Government, making full use of the Englishman's freedom of speech, and seldom abusing it.

Some did abuse it, of course. That was why several uniformed policemen were on the fringes of the crowd, listening, knowing which man was more likely to start using bad or abusive language, ready to quieten him down; knowing which man was likely to switch from criticism of the Government to criticism of the Royal Family, then go near enough to treasonable utterance to be warned. A warning was usually enough, for very few of these men were ever taken from their boxes by the police.

Mingling with the crowd, now several thousand strong, were half a dozen C.I.D. plainclothes men. This morning could become a pickpocket's harvest, and the best way to prevent it was to have C.I.D. men known to the thieves mixing with the crowd, as well as one or two who couldn't be identified.

The high-pitched voice of Little Willie became louder.

". . . and the lifeblood of this country is being sapped, that's what it is, being sapped by the worship of sport. Ess—pee—o—ah—tee, sport. I tell you again that the thought of millions of able-bodied men standing round a grass field and watching twenty-two men kicking a little ball about—"

"You ever played football, Willie?" a man called out.

"You ever been to a football match?"

If Willie said he had, the roar would be *hypocrite,* with a gust of laughter. If he said he hadn't, the roar would be *then what the hell do you know about it?* and another gust of laughter. But Willie was too old a hand to be caught so easily, and he spread his thin hands wide and waved his arms as he stood on the platform, spare and small and grey-haired.

"My information on this subject is taken from the highest authorities in the land," he retorted piercingly, "and the only thing I'd like to play football with is your head."

He won his laugh, but didn't join in with it. "Think, ladies and gentlemen, think. God gave you a mind, why don't you use it for once? Think about the awful iniquity of sport, consider how it is sapping the very lifeblood of our country. Export sales fall, prices rise, the working man wants more and more money, and why? I'll tell you why; *it's because of this worship of sport.*

Think, will you, just for a minute. Please! One million able-bodied men attend football matches every Saturday afternoon. Not a hundred, not a thousand, not a hundred thousand, but one million able-bodied men. Allow them one hour to reach the match, one hour to get home, two hours there, and that comes to four million working hours. Do you realise what kind of thing can be made in four million working hours? A hundred aeroplanes! An atomic pile! Enough clothes to dress a hundred thousand families! Thousands upon thousands of bicycles! A month's food for half of London. Think, ladies and gentlemen, I beg you to *think*. Pause only for a moment, and other tremendous advantages will occur to you, other commodities vital to the community which could be made by able-bodied men working for four million hours. You, madam – can *you* think of something? Can you imagine how much good—?"

A little woman standing next to a biggish man grinned and shook her head.

"Well, madam, what about your husband? I'm sure he—"

"I can tell you, Willie!" the husband shouted. "Four million bloody footballs, that's what they could make."

Gideon found himself chuckling as the crowd roared. Even Willie gave a half-hearted grin.

Gideon went on, towards Marble Arch itself, knowing that Kate would be here at any minute. He didn't want to keep her waiting, that happened often enough when it was unavoidable. Then an incident set his thoughts on to criminal parents and their children again. A woman, presumably the mother, struck a child of six or seven. It was a much more vicious blow than appeared justified by misbehaviour, and the child went white until colour began to flood his cheeks. But he did not cry. He did not protest. He did not even look up reproachfully, but turned and walked just ahead of the woman, his head bowed a little and thin shoulders bent. Obviously the child was used to being struck like that. Two couples stopped and looked as if they would protest, but the spiteful mother glared at them, their courage ebbed and they went on. Then a policeman stepped from the kerb towards her, and stood in front of her, solid and impassable.

She glared up. "What do you want?"

"What did you hit that child for?"

"None of your business," the woman retorted harshly. "I've got a right to correct my own child, I don't want no interference from you or no one else."

The woman was right, the policeman wrong, on legal grounds. Take a thing like this to court, even report it to the National Society for Prevention of Cruelty to Children, and what did words say? That a mother had smacked her child across the face for some trivial offence. A thousand mothers had probably slapped a thousand children that morning, and a thousand more would this afternoon. It was the way it was done, the glitter in the eyes, the cowed behaviour of the child, which made this incident different and justified the policeman – as a man but not as a police officer – in interfering. And it explained Gideon's surge of interest.

Obviously, the policeman wasn't quite sure how to handle the situation now, and a policeman should not allow his heart to rule his head. The two couples hovered near; encouraged by the law, they might join in the protest. Behind Gideon, Little Willie and the other speakers were still delivering their wisdom and their witticisms, and in front of him was this unexpected drama, watched almost pleadingly by the child, as if he were longing to say: "Don't make any fuss, please don't make any fuss."

"Listen, ma," the constable said, "I'd watch what I was doing, if I were you. It's one thing to punish a child, it's another to try to knock his head off. You be careful, or you'll find yourself in trouble one of these days."

The woman didn't speak, but dodged past him.

It was never possible to be sure whether the effect of such intervention would be good or bad. The woman might take it out of the child later; you could seldom find out what happened behind the closed doors and closed windows of the millions of homes which made up London.

Gideon caught up with the constable, who looked round, recognised him, and was immediately edgy; a man in his late twenties, Gideon saw, smaller than the old-style London policeman but fully trained in all the arts he needed in dealing with tough customers if not with spiteful mothers.

"Good morning, sir."

"'Morning," said Gideon. "Ever seen that woman and the kid before?"

"Oh, yes, sir, most Sundays."

"Regular, is she?"

"That's the third time I've seen her strike the child like that, and I couldn't let it go again, sir. I know that the book says—"

"Can't always follow the book, I know," said Gideon. "Ever talked to any of the other fellows about her?"

"No, sir."

"Does she always hit him out of the blue, like that?"

"I've never seen him do anything to deserve it," the constable said. "I could understand it if he got in her way, or started kicking stones about, but he just walks along and she hits him. Makes my blood boil."

"Children of your own?"

"Twins about the same age, as a matter of fact, sir."

"Hmm. Well, ask the other chaps if they've seen her hit him, and check where else she's been noticed."

The policeman's expression told its own story: that line of inquiry hadn't occurred to him.

"Lot of pocket-picking and bag-snatching about, I know, sir."

"Yes. If you get anything, report to the Division in the usual way."

"I will, sir."

"What's your name?" asked Gideon.

"Smith, sir, William Smith."

"I'll remember," Gideon said, and nodded and smiled, hoping that he had done enough to make sure that William Smith worked by regulation and not impulse. At least he was alive to the flood of petty crimes, now growing large enough to be important. There were many indications that children were being used.

Then Gideon saw his Kate coming towards him, tall and upright, and for once wearing a flowered dress, red on black, not the spotless white blouse and the dark skirt which had been almost a uniform for years. He'd heard much talk about this dress, but hadn't seen it before. It suited her, giving a touch of flamboyance. She was a fine-looking woman with a good figure, she walked well, and her face lit up when she saw him. That did a lot to take Gideon's mind off gloomier thoughts. They were not a demonstrative couple, but they touched hands and then fell into step.

"Sorry I'm late, George."

"Hardly a minute," Gideon said.

"I just missed a bus," Kate told him, and Gideon found himself looking at her handsome profile, the way the sun seemed to make her eyes gleam and her teeth glisten as she spoke, and the way it picked out the deep reds and unsuspected dark blues in the dress. "Are you finished at the office?"

"Yes, provided nothing new turns up," said Gideon. "I thought we'd go to Quag's for lunch."

"Oh, no, George! It's too expensive, we can easily go to the Corner House—"

"The Corner House, in that creation? We want somewhere to fit the dress!" Gideon said, and knew that he had pleased her. She didn't protest again, and so as to put the finishing touch to the day's celebration, Gideon waved a taxi down. Kate was laughing as she settled into the corner.

During lunch, he told her about the woman and the child, and she was much quicker on the uptake than the policeman had been.

"Do you think she might be training him as a pickpocket?"

"Could be. You're smart today."

"George," Kate said, "you've several unsolved murders on the books, and if you had a choice between solving them or finding

9

out if this child crime is organised or not, you'd forget the murders."

Gideon nodded, and asked: "Like to know something, Kate?"

"Yes."

"I'm going to know the answer to the increase in child crime this month, if I have to put every man at the Yard on to it."

"It'll be one thing finding out," Kate said, "quite another stopping it."

2

THE FIRST MONDAY

GIDEON went into his office a little before nine o'clock, next morning, in exactly the same way as he went in most mornings. He approached with slow and deliberate tread, knowing that his door was ajar, so that the two men inside could hear him coming; and he knew also that the Duty Sergeant in the hall had telephoned them to say he was on his way. He felt rather like a schoolmaster at a senior school, dealing with men who were intellectually on a par with him, but who were acutely conscious that he was boss. The fact that the two men inside, Lemaitre and Bodwin, had prepared a report on the week-end's events and were ready to be cross-examined on it, if need be, amused him mildly. It also pleased his vanity, which wasn't excessive.

Lemaitre, who had been on night duty for nearly a year and back on days as Gideon's chief *aide* only for a few weeks, looked up with a grin, and greeted him: "'Morning, George."

"Hallo, Lem. 'Morning, Bodwin."

"Good morning, sir."

"What's in this morning?" asked Gideon.

"As a matter of fact I think the weather must have softened everybody's heart, quietest week-end we've had for a long time," said Lemaitre. He was a tall, thin, rather bony man, who

11

grinned rather than smiled, was the ideal second-in-command and more than content to leave the real responsibility to Gideon and the senior Superintendents. "Usual crop of burglaries, bit of trouble out at Kempton Park on Saturday, some dips and a knifing, that's about all. Several reports from outside the area, though, I expect we'll be asked to send at least three chaps into the provinces, but that's not unusual."

Gideon was sitting down, at a big desk. He eased his collar without unfastening his tie.

"Hmm," he said, looking through the report, part of which was typewritten and part of which was in Lemaitre's almost copperplate handwriting. He ran his gaze down the pages and flipped them over. There were a number of arrest reports, none of them on major offences, a few reports on the week-end crimes, with no particular stress on child crime, notes about the provincial jobs where the Yard was likely to be called in, all of them murders.

"Anything fresh about the juvenile stuff?"

"No, sir, nothing that isn't down there."

"All right, you carry on." Bodwin went out, a middle-aged and grey-haired Sergeant with a bald patch, and the door closed silently behind him. Lemaitre went over to his own, smaller desk at the other side of the long, narrow room, with its three windows which overlooked the Embankment and the Thames. The weather on the Monday was as good as Sunday's, and the scene looked at its best.

"Good week-end, George?"

"So-so," said Gideon. "Spent yesterday morning here over the Riddall extradition job. I think the Spanish will play all right. How'd you get on?"

"I'm okay now," said Lemaitre quietly. "I'm cured."

He gave a grin which was more taut than usual, and almost belied his words. Lemaitre's wife had left him, nearly a year ago; the divorce was almost at the decree absolute stage. Now and again something Lemaitre did or said proved that he had not really recovered from this, although he knew as well as

Gideon that he was much better off without his wife. Now, he went off the subject almost too quickly. "I didn't put this in the report, George, it only came in twenty minutes ago, but you remember that old boy who died in the fire on Friday?"

Gideon looked up sharply.

"Henderson? Yes."

"He didn't die of suffocation in a fire."

"Well, well," said Gideon. "What was it?"

"Strangulation."

"We positive?"

"Clinton did the P.M. and checked with Grey."

"Clear case?"

"Pretty clear," said Lemaitre, "and a funny one, if you ask me." He sat on the corner of his desk and lit a cigarette – he was smoking much less than he had during the period of greatest strain, but still smoked plenty. "The old boy is left to look after himself for a couple of nights, his housekeeper goes to visit a sick friend, he gets strangled and someone tries to make it look as if he was suffocated by the smoke. That's a job for Syd Warr, I'd say."

"Yes," agreed Gideon thoughtfully. "I'll call the Division and fix it."

"If you ask me, all you've got to do is to bust that housekeeper's alibi wide open, and there you are," said Lemaitre. "She probably got tired of waiting for the eighty-year-old to die, and helped him on."

Gideon didn't comment.

"I know, I know," grinned Lemaitre, "here's this idiot Lemmy jumping to conclusions again. The truth is, George, I can't help it, it's part of my metabolism or what-have-you. I also know it's why I'll never rise higher than a C.I., but who cares?"

Gideon said half-seriously: "I care." He lifted the telephone. "Get me AI Division, please," he said to the operator, and rang off. "Now, we want the alibi checked, and the house searched again, Warr'd better go over right away and see what the Divisional reports about the outside of the house were like.

13

There were rumours that Henderson kept hundreds of pounds under his mattress and we can't find 'em – better make sure those rumours are checked too."

Then the telephone bell rang and Gideon spoke to the Superintendent at AI.

This was Gideon, at work.

Lemaitre had watched and listened to him on and off for ten years, and could still be absorbed. Gideon had a faculty of absolute concentration on the job in hand; and a gift, which had made him Commander, of being able to finish with one job and start the next almost without pausing to think. The years had trained him to keep every case in its own little pigeon-hole of his mind, a hole to be opened or closed at will. To the man standing by, it was fascinating, for Gideon now talked as if the murder of eighty-year-old Henderson was the only job which mattered; at that moment, it was.

He rang off, loosened his tie and let the ends hang over his chest, and then telephoned again.

"Hold it," Lemaitre interrupted, "there's another little prize-packet which I didn't put in the report, either."

"Anything much?"

Lemaitre paused, as if to relish the full flavour of the coming revelation.

"You may think so. You know Frisky Lee married a young popsie, and they have just become proud parents?"

Gideon went very still.

"Well?"

"Mother and child doing well," Lemaitre announced, "so well that Frisky's emigrating to Australia."

Gideon exploded: *"What?"*

"Thought that would touch you on the raw," Lemaitre said, grinning. "It's a fact. Hemmy told me himself. There's the biggest crook we've never been able to put inside going to the other side of the world to spend his ill-gotten gains. Good riddance, I say."

"When's he going?" Gideon asked, in a quiet voice.

"The end of the month," Lemaitre answered. "He's got his passage booked by sea, everything going to be sold up. Lyon is looking after his interests here." Lemaitre paused. "Dammit, George, it's not the whole world."

"If Frisky Lee gets out of England with a clean record, I'll hand in my resignation." Gideon sounded bleak enough to mean it.

"I knew you'd be shaken, but I didn't think you'd take it this way," Lemaitre said uneasily. "Why, Frisky's been on the level for years."

"You think he has."

"You've got Frisky on the brain," Lemaitre declared irritably. "Hemmy's more relieved than sorry, I know that much. Let Australia have him, that's what Hemmy says."

"No one's going to get Lee if I can keep him in England," Gideon said, and pulled up a telephone and talked to Hemmingway, of the NE Division, where Frisky lived in a house near Petticoat Lane.

Lemaitre, in a different mood, studied him closely. Gideon worrying a problem like the kid thieves was impressive if fatherly. Gideon seeking vengeance against such a man as Frisky Lee was uncompromising and almost frightening; a man who could hate.

Ten years ago, Frisky had been known as the biggest fence and cruellest man in London, utterly unscrupulous and utterly bad. He and Gideon had clashed a dozen times, and Lee might be said to represent Gideon's one great failure. Since the last clash, Lee had apparently run straight. He owned a chain of shops, mostly in London's East End, and much land, also. In Gideon's view, he was still financing the smaller fences, was still London's worst criminal.

Gideon said into the telephone: "That's it, Hemmy, get everything you can on Lee – —past and present. Check his wife's past, too. I'll get everything possible done here . . . What's that? . . . Well, if he's due to leave at the end of the month, we've little enough time, how about digging for a week?

15

Then I'll come and see you."

Apparently Hemmingway agreed.

Gideon rang off, to find Lemaitre apparently preoccupied with reports. For the first time since being told of Lee's plans, Gideon's expression eased into a smile, and he lifted the telephone again.

"Ask Superintendent Warr to come and see me, will you?" he asked the operator.

"Here we go," said Lemaitre, forgetting the reports. He stood up as another telephone on Gideon's desk rang; in all there were three. "Like me to take that, George?"

"No, I'll take it," Gideon said. "Little job for you. Check with AB, will you? They've a copper named William Smith, number 27532, who was on duty in Hyde Park yesterday. See if he put in a special report,"

"What about?"

"A woman and a child." The door began to open: this would be Warr, who had a funny trick of opening doors slowly, as if he wanted to hear what was being said, and was afraid that it would not be to his credit. Few people really liked Warr, except elderly women, and they doted on him; more defrauding housekeepers owed their prison sentences to Warr than any other single factor in London. "Just ask Percy to let me know if Smith did put in a report," Gideon added.

"Okay." Lemaitre picked up a telephone, and belatedly Gideon picked up his. Warr came in. He was a biggish, plumpish, pale man, with pink cheeks and blue eyes, a kind of unctuous look. One could imagine him with a religious tract in his hand, saying gentle things to soothe his congregation; or imagine him as a country solicitor, or a minor municipal official, always giving the soft answer to turn away wrath. Above all, he could be pictured as a doctor with a bedside manner to beat them all.

"Hallo, Syd," Gideon greeted, "have a look at that." He pushed over the notes he had made, then spoke briskly into the telephone: "Gideon here, sorry to keep you." He picked up a pencil and began to write: "Yes, I got that . . . Yes. I'll come in as soon as I'm through with the job I've got on now, the Henderson business . . . well, I should think they could wait a day or two down at Dover, we can always send someone down in a hurry if needs be, but the other jobs ought to be dealt with right away . . . Yes, I'll come in a minute." He rang off, finished his notes, and looked up at Warr, who stood there in his suit of clerical grey, reading, lips pursed. "Which would you rather do, Syd? Tackle this job, or have a few days in Chester?"

"The body in the barrel job?"

"Yes."

"If it's all the same to you, I'll stay home."

"Right. Know anything about the Henderson business?"

"You may not believe it," said Warr in his soft voice, "but I had a premonition that you'd want me to look into that, when I heard that Henderson was strangled. Any special instructions?"

"Just get stuck into it."

"Right you are," said Warr, and tore the note off Gideon's pad. "May I take this?"

"Help yourself!"

Warr smiled, Lemaitre scowled as he put down the receiver and Warr went out almost as stealthily as he had come in. The door closed. Gideon stood up, and began to fiddle with the ends of his tie. The Assistant Commissioner wanted him, and while he could look as homely as he wished at his own desk, one tied one's tie for the A.C. and the passages.

"Percy tell you anything?" Gideon asked. "Make a note for me, the Old Man—"

"No, no special report," said Lemaitre. "That Warr! How did he know?"

"Know what?"

"Don't be dumb, George. How did he know that Henderson had been strangled?"

"He keeps his ears open."

"Sly devil," Lemaitre said, in an almost grumbling tone. "If he can get in by the back door, he will. Good job he's not a crook. What's the Old Man want? Out-of-town jobs?"

"Yes."

"I'll tell you what, George," Lemaitre said, as Gideon finished knotting his tie, and stepped to the door," if we're not careful, we'll be in a jam. We've already got two chaps out in the country, and if the Old Man wants another three, we'll be too short-handed for safety. Why don't you try to put a couple of them off?"

Gideon said easily: "The day we tell the provincial chaps that we can't spare two or three men to help them out, we'll begin to put up the shutters. But I know what you mean – whenever we get short-handed, something big always crops up. Such as working on Lee before he goes to Australia."

"You want to know what I think?" demanded Lemaitre, as Gideon opened the door.

Gideon grinned. "You think I'm crazy to worry about Lee, and it's a hangover from the day he fingered his nose at me. You think I'm soft about those kids. And you're damned sure these so-and-so country coppers could do the job perfectly well themselves, they only call us in because it looks like being long and tedious, or else someone's going to get a kick in the pants and better us than them. And you want to know why we don't let them handle their own jobs more, and stew in their own juice. Every time we send 'em a man, it looks as if they've got us on the end of a string. I'll be seeing you."

He went out and closed the door.

"George," said Lemaitre weakly to its panels, "one of these days someone's going to kick you up the pants." He turned to his desk, and as he did so, a telephone bell rang on Gideon's. Lemaitre swung towards that, and a bell on his own desk rang. "Here we go," he said resignedly.

"Four ears and four eyes wouldn't be enough in this office. Which one shall I answer first?"

He answered Gideon's.

"Lemaitre speaking."

"Excuse me, Mr. Lemaitre," said the Hall Sergeant in his

unmistakable voice, "do you think Mr. Gideon's particularly busy this morning?"

"Why?"

"Well, there's an old woman—there's a lady here, asking to see him. She says she wants to see him in person, and no one else will do. I've tried to fob her off, but I can't do a thing. Says something about her daughter being missing, and she looks as if she's in a bad way. I thought if Mr. Gideon wasn't up to his neck in it—" The Sergeant paused, hopefully.

"I expect he'll see her," Lemaitre prophesied. "Tell her it might be an hour, though, he's at a conference."

"I don't think she'll mind waiting," the hall Sergeant said. "Thanks a lot, sir."

Lemaitre banged the receiver down while his own bell was still ringing, and let it ring long enough to make a shorthand note; then he lifted the receiver and cut off the sound.

"Lemaitre."

"Jackson, KI Division," a man said briskly. "We've just had a bank hold-up. Two bank clerks were injured trying to stop the getaway. Looks like a thirteen thousand pounds job. I'm going over myself, but we're short of fingerprint men today, can you send someone over?"

Lemaitre wanted to say: Why the hell don't you handle it yourself?

Gideon would say: "Yes, right away."

"Sure, right away," said Lemaitre. "Got everything else you want?" Jackson was the last man in the world to suspect that there was any sarcasm in that question. "That's good, good-bye." He rang off, and immediately put in a call to Fingerprints, muttering as he waited: "Lap dogs to the Divisions and the provinces, that's what we are. Lap dogs. Hallo, Micky? . . . send a Sergeant and anyone else you've got hanging around doing nothing to KI, will you? . . . bank job, better look snappy." He grinned. "Yes, Mr. Finn, I'll tell him." He rang off, made a note on his desk, and sat back for the first time since Gideon had left the office.

Downstairs, a woman waited, anguished because her child was missing.

In the Divisions, the week's work was really getting under way.

Gideon had set aside his thoughts on the juvenile problem, and was agreeing with the Assistant Commissioner about which Superintendents to send out to the provinces. He would soon be briefing each man, who would choose his own *aides*. It was routine, even though each job had something different and had to be taken on its merits. The daily grind. It began to absorb Gideon, Lemaitre, Warr, and everyone else who had a specific job to do. Being absorbed, they stopped thinking about the other things, the things that might be happening, the crimes which hadn't yet been committed, or hadn't yet been reported. There was nothing new, and yet everything was new.

There was the school for pickpockets and bag-snatchers, for instance, being run under the noses of the police, on the south side of the river. There was Frisky Lee and his beautiful young wife, preparing for their new life in Australia.

And not very far from Scotland Yard, a girl in her early twenties was frightened for her life.

3

CAUSES OF FEAR

"REGGIE," this girl was saying, "put the knife away. You don't know what you're doing. Put the knife away."

The young man smiled at her.

It was not a cruel smile, and there was even compassion and gentleness in it. He was a handsome youth, and his looks as well as his veneer of culture had first attracted her to him. She had few friends, and her parents were dead. Her life had been aimless; a little travel, a little work if it suited her, a few charity committees, many acquaintances. She had met Reggie on a Mediterranean cruise, two months ago, and the cruise had given her the happiest three weeks of her life. She had felt so sure of him and his love, had felt a deep sense of security.

She had married him.

She was a bride of two weeks.

"Reggie," she said, with a sob in her voice, "put the knife away. Darling, don't stand there looking at me like that, put the knife away."

He stood holding the knife, smiling, unmoving. He was between her and the door of the small service flat in the heart of London – a flat rented with her money, although she did not realise it. Everything was done with her money, and she had been aware from the beginning that he *might* be marrying her for it, but this—this was a nightmare.

Nightmare.

"Reggie, please put that knife away."

The advertisement which they had answered about this flat had stressed: Soundproof. Constructed by the very latest methods. Absolutely quiet and secluded from the neighbours above, at the side, and below.

They'd talked about it, often; and never heard a sound, not even a radio turned up too loud.

The girl was pale as death.

"Reggie!"

It was a knife with a broad blade; a game knife. The sun came in at the window of the living-room, and glinted on the steel, especially on the edge where it had been sharpened, to give it a perfect cutting edge. He held it quite loosely, not as a dagger, but as if he would thrust it forward gently, piercing the flesh with the sharp point. He stood two feet away from his wife as she stood against the wall of the tiny kitchen, and she could not look away from the knife, so did not see the expression in his eyes.

"Reggie," she said brokenly, "you don't know what you're doing. Put—please put that knife away. I'll do anything you like, I'll give you anything, but put that knife away. *Please—*"

Reggie lowered the hand with the knife, and then put them into his pocket and drew the hand out, empty. His wife's relief was so great that for a few seconds she could only stand shivering despite the warmth of the day, looking at him as he continued to smile at her. A strange thing seemed to be happening, now; his mouth was working as if he was on the point of crying. He didn't cry, but moved slowly away from her, into the living-room. Beyond was the bathroom and the bedroom, and beyond that the soundproof walls. He walked stiffly, keeping his hand away from his pocket. He went out, closing the door behind him slowly, although it snapped.

The girl felt herself trembling, and leaned against the small dresser to keep herself upright.

"Reggie," she said in a choky voice, and her voice began to quiver. "You can't be—"

She didn't finish.

She made herself move towards a chair and drop down, burying her face in her hands, too weak to think at first; but it was not long before she began to think and fear and feel again.

The flat was silent.

Soundproof!

She stood up, staring towards the door, which Reggie had closed so firmly. She reached it, and touched the handle, but for a moment was almost too frightened to try to turn it. Then she did turn it, and pulled, but it didn't open. She pulled again and again, but it would not budge, and she knew the truth although she would not admit it to herself. He had locked her in.

"Reggie!" she screamed. "Let me out of here! Let me out!"

The door did not open.

Soon she gave up tugging and crying, and went to the window. This was a corner apartment, and it had one great disadvantage which she had not realised before; the windows overlooked the blank walls of another building. All she could see was the distorted shapes of the windows of the six floors below her.

The ground seemed a long way off.

She leaned out.

It would be impossible to climb down, absolutely impossible; she would fall to her death against the concrete below. If only Reggie—

She heard the door open, and swung round. He came in, briskly, smiling, almost gay. The strange look in his eyes was gone, and he had changed his suit for a pair of flannels and a jacket. He rubbed his hands together and said briskly: "I'm famished, pet, aren't you?"

She gaped at him.

"Come on, pet, don't look at me as if I were a ghost," said Reggie. "I'm famished. Marriage does something to me, I get

23

hungrier than when I was single, and do I sleep in the afternoon! I must have slept for a couple of hours today. How about some of that cake and extra thin bread and butter you're so good at?"

His bride said gaspingly: "Yes, yes, darling, of course. I won't be long, I'll put a kettle on." She swung round towards the electric stove, snatched up the kettle and filled it, splashing the water over herself, the stove, the floor.

While her back was turned towards him, his smile was not nice.

When she turned to look at him, it was charming.

She did not understand him, and did not know what to do. He was ill, of course, mentally ill; one of those people with two minds. No, not two minds, split minds. The ordeal was sapping her own intelligence, she was unable to think clearly, and hardly knew what to do as she fetched the butter from the larder, then the cake, then the bread. She took a bread knife out of the drawer, and began to slice the bread. Then she saw him looking at the light shimmering on the blade, and she cried out, and almost dropped it.

"Careful," Reggie said, "you'll cut yourself."

That was Eve Dennis and her husband, Reggie.

Marion Lane was very happy, although she was not married yet; and wouldn't be for an hour or so. She was still Miss Marion Lane, and had expected to be Miss Lane for a long time, but Robert had literally swept her off her feet. They had met at a dance run by the tennis club. In an old-time waltz he had swung her round and whirled and pirouetted until she had been breathless, and dazed with excitement. Life hadn't been quite the same since then, the pace had been so much faster than she was used to. Oddly, the tennis club itself had brightened her existence a great deal before she had met Robert. Clubs were wonderful for young girls who had no close relations, and certainly none at all who mattered; and she wasn't bad at tennis.

With her parents she had left the north of England for London six years ago, and afterwards, life had been dullish for several years. She had not needed to work, for her parents had been comfortably off, and her mother had also some money in her own right. Church socials, church meetings, a little committee work for the church and for charities, the occasional garden fete and Christmas Party hadn't exactly been exciting. Rather like Eve Dennis's life. The death of her parents within a few days of each other from virulent influenza had first stunned and then numbed her, and she had lived aimlessly for a year, keeping on the house and letting the top half to an elderly couple. Then at last she had joined the tennis club. From that moment it seemed just a breath or two away to Robert, dancing, courtship and this, her wedding day. She was as thrilled and excited as she believed a bride ought to be, a little sorry only because it was not to be a white wedding, but in a registry office, with a few friends. As if a wedding dress made any difference!

She was alone for half an hour now, her one close friend and would-have-been bridesmaid had gone out to get some oddments needed for the ceremony. That was to be at two o'clock, and it was already nearly twelve.

Marion wasn't yet dressed, but she had bathed and a dressing gown was loose about her. She felt warm, her body flushed with the hot water and with the heat of the day. Her cheeks were flushed, too, and her blue eyes seemed unusually bright.

She had the oddest feeling.

Alone, in the large room downstairs, which had once been the drawing-room and was now her bedroom, she found herself studying her reflection in the long mirror of the wardrobe. Her bare feet looked pink; her hands, her face and throat did, also. She found herself easing the dressing gown back a little from the front, found herself slipping the gown off, feeling strangely guilty. She looked at her fair, flushed young body, and imagined Robert, just behind her; Robert coming close.

Then she heard a car draw up outside, and thrust her arms into the sleeves again. By the time Ethel had arrived, she was in bra and girdle.

Ethel was five years older, plain, angular, and too thin. She came in briskly.

"You'll have to hurry or you'll keep him waiting," she said. "I don't know that it would do him any harm, but registrars don't like it."

"Oh, I'll be on time!"

"So I should think," said Ethel, and then seemed to be struck by the sight of her friend's reflection in the dressing-table mirror, and move slowly towards her. "Marion," she went on quietly, "you look lovely, I must say that."

"Oh, don't be ally."

"I'm not one for paying compliments," Ethel declared, "but you look really lovely." Then she moved abruptly. "If a girl's not looking at her best on her wedding day, when will she? But *do* hurry, dear."

"I'll be in plenty of time, you're fussing too much."

They didn't speak for several minutes after that; and said nothing of significance until Marion had put on her dress, and Ethel was zipping up the back. The dress was tight-fitting, and showed the rounded curves of her breasts beautifully. It was high at the neck, and of a shiny blue taffeta, just the shade she had fancied. It also brought out the blue in her eyes. She stood in front of the mirror while Ethel zipped, and as she let the zip go, Ethel said abruptly: "Marion?"

"Yes?"

"You're quite sure, aren't you?"

"Of loving Robert ? Of course."

"Marion, you do feel absolutely sure of him, don't you?" Ethel spoke so quickly that the words seemed to be gabbled. "After all, you haven't known him very long and no one knows a lot about him. I agree that he seems all right. I like him myself, but marrying a stranger doesn't seem right, somehow.

And he has no relatives. *Are* you sure?"

Marion turned round.

"You've asked me this several times, dear, and I can only give the same answer. I'm absolutely positive. Don't worry. I shall be very, very happy."

"Before you put on your make-up, you'd better have a sandwich and something to drink," Ethel said gruffly. "You won't want to make a mess of your lipstick afterwards, and there isn't much more than an hour to go."

"Of course I'm sure," Marion said to herself; "I'm absolutely sure. I couldn't want anyone better than Robert."

Robert Carne left his one-roomed flat for the ceremony, half an hour before it was due, and walked briskly, as if without a care in the world. He looked nearer thirty than his forty-one years, his lean figure helped that appearance of youthfulness, and there was a curious little smile at his lips, attractive to most people. His curly hair was thinning a little, but that did not really age him. He wore a beautifully cut suit of navy blue.

A Police Sergeant in plainclothes, who happened to come out of a tobacconist's shop where he had been making some fruitless inquiries about the bank raid that morning, saw Carne, and watched him without appearing to.

"Where've I seen that chap before?" he wondered.

He could not call it to mind, and could not give Carne a name; all he knew was that there was a certain familiarity, and that he associated it, vaguely, with his work. He saw Carne hail a taxi, but did not hear his directions to the driver. Had he heard " . . . registry office" he might have recollected where he had seen Carne before, and might possibly have stopped or at least delayed the wedding. For recollection would have told him that he had seen Carne in connection with the death of his, Came's, wife, by food poisoning. That had been two years ago. The Sergeant had been a rookie then, and still had to learn to use his mind like a camera and his memory like a card index.

So he got on a bus and went to the Yard to report negatively.

The Assistant Commissioner for Crime at New Scotland Yard was a tall, lean, astute-looking Lieutenant-Colonel, with a fine war record and considerable administrative experience. Gideon knew him well and trusted him; and he was shrewd enough to know that although Gideon wanted action of the Henderson business, his chief preoccupation was with Frisky Lee.

"Any objection if I put a couple of men on to checking everything we can about Frisky?" Gideon asked.

"Go ahead."

"Thanks."

"And while you're here, what about these young kids?" the A.C. asked. "The Home Office wants a comprehensive report on all child shoplifters and pickpockets caught in the past six months."

"They like it tonight?" Gideon asked abruptly.

"In the next few weeks."

Gideon grinned. "They could really have it tonight. I'd dress it up for 'em."

He went out, satisfied that he could do whatever he thought best, and now wondering whether he was letting the old failure against Lee rankle enough to distort his own judgment. Everything about Lee was phoney; even his nickname; he was called Frisky because of his trick of absolute stillness.

Gideon briefed three Superintendents for the provincial jobs, then detailed two older men, an Inspector and a Detective-Sergeant, to work on the Lee probe, co-operating whenever practicable with Hemmingway of NE Division. Then Gideon went back to his office. He pulled his tie apart again, and stepped to the window, which was wide open. He pushed it up another fraction of an inch. The morning was warming up, the sun seemed to reflect too brightly from the Thames, the smell of petrol was stronger than ever, the first whiff of a London summer's perfume. He turned back to his desk, and looked at several notes which Lemaitre had put there, stopping longest at the report that a woman was waiting for him downstairs. He had come in at a side entrance, or would probably have seen the Hall Sergeant, and been told about this before.

Gideon called the hall, and the Sergeant answered.

"Hallo, Joe, that woman still waiting?"

"Patient as a midwife, Mr. Gideon."

"What name did she give?"

"Crow."

"What?"

"Crow."

"Hmm. Get anything out of her?"

"As a matter of fact, she doesn't seem to know much herself," the Sergeant said. "If she hadn't insisted on asking for you, and if I didn't know you like to see anyone who does, I'd have put her off."

"How old is she?"

"'Bout fifty."

"What type?"

"Lower middle-class, sir, I'd say."

"Where is she?"

"In the lower waiting-room."

"I'll come down," said Gideon, adjusting his tie again. "Don't tell her I'm on the way."

"No, sir," the Sergeant said, and he sounded much more cheerful.

Lemaitre was still busy taking down the message. Gideon went out, walked along to the lift, then decided to use the stairs. He went steadily, head jutting forward, pondering over everything he'd done and heard that morning, until he reached the ground floor. Then he switched to the thought of the woman who was waiting for him. His name was in the newspapers more than any other officer at the Yard, and it wasn't unusual for people to ask for him personally. The Sergeant and others on duty could usually scent the curious-minded and the gossips, and Gideon was seldom worried by them. Acquaintances, both of his own and of his family,

JOHN CREASEY

sometimes called, some trading on their acquaintance, hoping for special consideration for themselves or for friends in trouble. If Mrs. Crow was one of those, two minutes would be enough.

Gideon went straight to the waiting-room. It had a window through which he could see inside, although to anyone inside it looked like frosted glass. The woman was sitting leaning back against the wall in an attitude of utter dejection and dismay. Gideon studied her face; she was a stranger.

She looked possessed by fear.

Gideon went in.

She jumped up, a woman of fifty, perhaps a little younger, grey-haired, dressed in a too thick tweed suit made by a good tailor, wearing good quality gloves and shoes, carrying a good quality leather handbag.

"I'm sorry to have kept you waiting, Mrs. Crow," Gideon said, and smiled to try to reassure her. "How can I help you?"

At first, she couldn't find words; she had waited for over an hour for this moment, and now it had come, was speechless. Gideon did not try to hurry her, but sat on the corner of a square table, quite relaxed, and hoping that his manner would soon soothe her.

"I—I know I shouldn't have asked for you, but—but I've heard such wonderful things about you, Mr. Gideon, and—and no one seems to be able to help. They mean well, I know they mean well, but no one seems to understand that Sheila's missing. She's all I've got left, and I'm sure he's taken her away." She closed her burning eyes, swayed, but then squared her shoulders and went on doggedly: "I'm sorry if I'm being emotional. I'm talking about my daughter Sheila, of course. She is only six. Her father always swore that he'd take her away from me, although the court gave me custody of her. She went to see him last night, and she hasn't come back. She—"

"If she's with your ex-husband, we'll soon find out," Gideon assured her. "You've nothing to fear if the court gave you custody. Now, tell me more about it." He pressed a bell, to

30

bring in a note-taker who would write down everything Mrs. Crow said.

This was a cause of fear he could really understand.

It would have been easy to have left her with a Sergeant, when the note-taker arrived. Staying with them cost him fifteen minutes and gained him a closer study of Mrs. Crow. She wasn't fifty or anywhere near it, he decided; probably in the late thirties. Worry, anxiety, fear, and a night without sleep, had conspired to make her look much older than she was. Ten years ago, she had probably been quite striking; now she was grey, jaded, faded.

The story of the past few years of her life came out quietly once she realised that Gideon meant to give her a thorough hearing. An unfaithful husband, drink, quarrels: she had "stuck it out" because of Sheila, had believed that Sheila might yet mend the marriage. Then her husband, John Crow, had brought a young girl to the house, as a "maid"; that had been going beyond endurance.

Divorce, custody of the child, the court's permission for the father to see the child once a month – always the first Sunday in the month.

Yesterday.

The day a shrew of a woman had struck a boy not much older than Sheila, and sent him on, cowed and afraid.

"And she isn't back, Mr. Gideon. I waited until midnight, as my ex-husband said that she was on her way, then I went to his flat. It was all in darkness and no one was there. I'm sure he's taken her away. I'm sure he's going to try to take her out of the country, too, he always said that he would take her abroad if he had half a chance."

She was really in despair.

She had gone to her local police station and been soothed by a policewoman, then by a Night Superintendent who had promised to look into the matter, and had sent her home; she had dropped into a sleep of exhaustion, not waking until ten o'clock.

"And the police round the corner still couldn't tell me anything, so I just felt that I had to come to the fountain head. I *had* to. I've heard so much about you."

"If I can help I will," Gideon promised. "I'll make sure nothing's been reported about your ex-husband, if you'll wait for a few minutes."

Gratitude momentarily drove out fear.

"Oh, I'll wait as long as you like!"

Gideon went out to the nearest telephone, and called Superintendent Carter, of CD Division, where Mrs. Crow lived. It was one of central London's most densely populated districts.

"Have you been out to see that man Crow?" Gideon asked.

Carter, dry-voiced and laconic, said promptly: "So Mrs. Crow carried out her threat, did she? I hope you played nicely for her, George. Crow's not home, and I'm waiting for a report from his office now. He hasn't been there yet. If he's still not there when we go again—"

"We'll be after him," Gideon said. "Thanks." He rang off, called Information, and arranged for a teletype message to go to all ports and airports with a description of Crow and his daughter. He didn't relish the idea of Crow laughing at him from a ship or an aircraft. If the couple were intercepted anywhere, they would be held long enough for the police on the spot to get in touch with the Yard.

Then he went back to the waiting-room.

"Mrs. Crow," he said, "we've decided to watch all ports and airfields and make quite sure that your daughter isn't taken out of the country. Please don't worry about that. But there is something you can do to help."

Her eyes lit up again.

"Just tell me what it is!"

"Talk to the newspapers about this, and give them the latest photograph of your daughter. They'll be glad to print it and to help."

"Oh, I will, and I've a photograph here—"

Gideon took her to the "back room" where an Inspector

handed out news to the Press. Several Fleet Street men were always inside, or just out on the Embankment, hoping pessimistically for the latest sensation. News, especially in the crime field, was slack; in that way Mrs. Crow was lucky, for she would get plenty of space.

"All you must say at this stage is that your daughter is missing. Don't accuse your husband, don't say anything about him threatening to leave the country," Gideon said. "Just stick to the known facts." He winked over Mrs. Crow's grey head to the Back Room Inspector, shook hands with the woman, and went back to his office.

The job started him thinking about children, and he could not get the child of Hyde Park out of his mind. Why had that woman struck the boy so savagely?

Where was he now?

Was she training him, by fear, to become a thief?

Somehow, finding where the two of them were, and what they were doing, had become a fixed purpose in Gideon's mind, part of the major task of learning the truth about the crop of child criminals. Yet no children had been caught or reported since the middle of last week, and most of the cases in the juvenile courts had been dealt with. It was almost as if he was beating the air.

But he knew better.

Quick Joe Mann was sixty-two, and had spent twenty-one years in prison. There had been few cleverer pickpockets in his time, but it was six years since he had last come out of jail, and since then he was believed to have run straight.

He lived with one of his three married daughters, in QR Division, over the river from Scotland Yard, and this married daughter had several young children of her own, each nicely-behaved and brought up to be strictly honest. Quick Joe, his daughter and his grandchildren, had all been considered in Gideon's search for those who taught the children to steal, but the Divisional reports had given the family a clean bill.

The reports omitted one fact.

Quick Joe's daughter was a seamstress, and took in work from small manufacturers – and from time to time, other women came, to work for her for a day or so or a week or so; all part-timers. Others again came with the dresses and lingerie for finishing, so there was a constant stream of women, mostly in the thirties and forties, and all apparently on their lawful occasions.

There was no reason why the QR Divisional police should know that each woman had at least one child of an easily teachable age.

The same women seldom came more than six or seven times, and among those who had ceased coming was a Mrs. Wray, who had one son, Peter; the boy whom Gideon had seen in Hyde Park.

4

AT HOME

THE child, Peter Wray, was "at home".

Home was a top room in a house near Whitechapel which should have been condemned years ago, and would be, before long. Meanwhile, people lived there. The mass of Londoners moved about the city and the suburbs, in wealthy homes, middle-class homes and poor ones, in tenements and luxury flats, in large hotels and in little hotels, in dingy back streets, but in all of these there was a measure of cleanliness. Home was home. Here and there black spots remained, and Gideon and all the police knew of these and also knew what was bred in them, but could do nothing except to try to help the National Society for the Prevention of Cruelty to Children whenever any cases of abuse of children were found. Gideon knew as well as the next man that ill-treatment of children was not confined to the very poor, but experience proved beyond doubt that slums were conducive to neglect.

It was part of London life.

Peter Wray, then, was "at home".

He was standing in a dark, airless cupboard. He could lean to one side, or forwards and backwards. He was very small, so there was just sufficient room for him even to lie down on the floor. The only light came through the sides of the door, which was locked. Sometimes he could hear movement in the room beyond, and sometimes there was silence, and he did not know which to fear most. Silence meant that his mother was out, and if she was out there was no hope of the door opening and of being released; similarly, there was no fear that the door would open and she would beat him.

He was hungry.

He was thirsty.

His head ached.

His body ached.

Suddenly, he heard a sound, and grew tense and began to tremble. The door of the room outside opened, and he heard it close again, quietly. Now he tried to stop trembling, and to listen. It was often possible to tell what his mother would be like before she had said a word. If she walked heavily, and stumbled, that was best, because then she was drunk and when she was drunk she was almost kind. She was only drunk when she was in the money.

The door closed quietly; that was an ominous sign.

Peter held his breath.

Then, he heard her stumble. A chair scraped. He twisted round and looked towards the blackness of the door, not knowing that he was praying that it would open. He could actually hear her heavy breathing. He knew that often she would come in and flop down on her bed or into a chair, and drop off to sleep and not wake up for hours. Of all the things that could happen, that was the worst. He clenched and raised his hands. If he tapped at the door and she heard him, she might let him out; but she might be so furious that she would open the door, beat him savagely, then slam it on him and lock him in again. If she did that, it would be for the whole night through.

The chair scraped, and there were more footsteps. The boy twisted up his face, gritted his teeth, and rested his clenched hand on the door, but he did not tap, for his mother was coming nearer. She might have remembered he was here, and be coming to open the door. If she thought he was trying to hurry her, she might not come at all.

She was going to come; he could hear her fumbling! The key turned.

Now he had a kind of excitement, fed on hope, that she would be in a good mood. That would be freedom from fear for a little while, and might also mean food.

Light came, making him screw up his eyes against it, and although he could smell his mother's nearness, even to the gin on her breath, he could not really see. Then his vision cleared, and he saw that she was moving away from the door, which meant that he could step out. He crept forward very slowly, watching her closely, looking for the tell-tale signs on her face. If her lips were tight and thin it was a bad sign. If she was smiling—

She was smiling!

"Watcher, me little ole wage-earner," she greeted. "Learned your lesson this time, 'ave yer?"

"Y—y—yes," he stammered.

"Well, let's 'ave it."

"I must not talk to strangers in the street."

"You said it. Try again."

"I must not talk to strangers in the street."

"Now there's a bright boy," his mother approved, gustily. "Don't say your old ma don't give credit where credit's doo. Now you go across the landing and pee, and then come and get the bag for some fish an' chips. I'm in the money, Pete ole boy, we're going to eat like kings today. Fred's is open, I just passed it. Didn't dare go in meself, you know what a robber Fred is, with me in my condition he would have given me short change. Never trust no one, that's my motter. Now get a move on, or I'll slap you across the ear-'ole in a way you won't forget."

Peter skipped out.

He came hurrying back, his eyes bright, his tiredness and aching limbs almost forgotten, eagerness in his manner. They were going to have fish and chips, his mother would be all right

tonight.
He was happy.

At the Yard, it was a fairly quiet day. The Crow Case was the main one. There was no trace of the father and daughter, and the newspapers were making this bigger news than a smash and grab, the bank robbery, and the hundred and one little crimes which had been committed. Gideon did not nag Hemmingway about Frisky Lee; by Sunday, his report would be in, positive or negative, and Gideon had learned not to allow any case to destroy his detachment; not even the reports on the wave of child crimes for the Home Office. He was not convinced that the wave was subsiding, although undoubtedly there was a lull.

Of the dozen or more cases where children had been caught, five were identical in one respect: the children had been scared into admitting that they had been taught by their mothers, with the knowledge of their fathers. Of course all the parents denied it, none had a record, and it was worrying to think that each was expert enough to teach specialist crimes like picking pockets and snatching handbags, yet were unknown to the police.

The obvious explanation was that the mothers were teaching at second hand.

Gideon made a note to find out if these five mothers had any common association with known criminals, and passed it on to Lemaitre.

Gideon left his office and reached the courtyard which was dark in the shadows because the evening sunlight struck the tall buildings surrounding it. A car turned in slowly. Seeing Warr at the wheel, Gideon waited. Warr hadn't telephoned and hadn't sent for any help, he was one of the self-sufficient ones. He rubbed his pale, plump hands together in a characteristic gesture, and smiled blandly at Gideon.

"Good evening, George."
"How'd it go, Syd?"

"Do you know, I wouldn't like to say," said Warr. "I've spent a lot of time with Henderson's housekeeper, Mrs. Smallwood, and while I doubt whether the woman has the highest moral standards, I'm not at all sure that she strangled the old man. There were three hundred and twenty-seven pounds under his mattress."

"Who says so?"

"She does."

"How'd she know?"

"He trusted her so much that he asked her to count it, only two days before he died."

"She tell anyone?"

Warr gave a little laugh, quite free from pose, and for a moment was almost likeable.

"You don't take long, George, do you? That's the angle I'm after, but I can't say that I've found anything yet."

"How about her alibi?"

"So-so. It could be broken, I think, she wasn't very far away. She couldn't have walked to Henderson's place and back from the friend she was staying with, but she could have cycled and could have taken a taxi or used a car. I've got the Division doing that donkey work."

Gideon grinned.

"Go and tell Lemaitre that, it'll cheer him up."

"I'll tell him if I see him. Are you going home?"

"Yes."

"What it is to be the boss," sighed Warr. "I'll be here for three hours yet. Don't let me keep you." He went off, padding up the steps, and it was impossible to be sure whether he meant to be sour or not. Gideon put the information into the relevant pigeon-hole in his mind, and promptly forgot it. No one else stopped him. The nightly peak of London's rush hour was over, but there was still plenty of traffic. Policemen on point-duty saluted as he drove along in his black Humber Hawk with its specially-tuned engine. He wanted to ruminate, and could do that best at home. With luck he would see most of the television programme tonight, and it was surprising how often some elusive factor in a case came to him as he watched. He would just have time to give the grass a run-over, too, while Kate was getting supper.

Near Hurlingham, in the south-west of London where he had his home, he passed a Detective-Sergeant cycling in the other direction. The man recognised him and raised a hand from the handlebars.

In a way that salute started a chain of events.

The cycling Sergeant's name was Arkwright, from AI Division. He had a kind of roving commission, and had been making inquiries in the tobacconist's shop that morning when he had seen a spruce-looking young man whom he hadn't been able to place. It would not be true to say that the identity of the man had teased Arkwright all day, but he had wondered about it several times, and had actually been thinking of him five minutes earlier. Then he had seen a black Humber Hawk coming towards him, and like every one of London's C.I.D. men, seeing a similar car, had thought: "That might be Gideon." Gideon was a man one liked to notice, because it was a good thing to be noticed by him.

"Well, he's got a night off," Arkwright said, and shrugged, and settled down to cycling even faster. He drove a police car during the day but for private life used a bicycle, being a bachelor, young enough to enjoy the exercise, and sensible enough to know that one day he would be glad of the money he saved. His mind was very much on Gideon as he turned off the main road and headed north, intending soon to turn west and so head for his lodgings.

Then he exclaimed: "Got it!"

Gideon had been the *open sesame* to his mind, for a little over two years ago Gideon had questioned him after he himself had questioned the spruce-looking man. Now Arkwright remembered everything. He had interrogated the spruce-looking man about the death of his young and pretty wife, but it had been largely a formality, because the doctor's certificate had been quite clear. There had been a short, sharp epidemic of food poisoning in the district at that time, which had been traced to an infected batch of meat pies.

So Arkwright, having remembered, promptly put the recollection out of his mind.

He would not have done so had he even suspected that the man he had recognised now used a different name: the name of Robert Carne. When his pretty young wife had died of food poisoning in a North London suburb, he had been known as Roger Clayton.

Roger Clayton, *alias* Robert Carne, had thought it unwise to tell his new bride that he had been married not once but twice before, and it did not occur to Marion Carne *née* Lane that he had been. At half-past six that evening, just when Gideon got home, they were in a hotel room at Brighton, overlooking the sea and the two piers, and seeing more people on the beach and in the water than was usual on an August day. On the south coast, everyone who could jumped at the chance given by the spring "heat-wave", and although the water was stinging cold, one forgot that after the first shock was over.

Carne stood by the window.

His bride came out of the bathroom, where she had been setting out the toilet things, and stood still and looked at him. She loved the shape of the back of his head and neck. She loved the way his small ears pressed close to the side of his head. She loved the upright way in which he stood, and the squareness of his shoulders. She did not move towards him at once, and he turned round slowly, obviously aware that she was watching. He smiled; and to Marion that was a perfect smile, making him look unbelievably handsome. She could not understand why he should have fallen in love with her.

"Hallo, sweet. Finished the chores?"

"Yes." Her voice was a little husky.

"Come and have a look at the view," he said.

She joined him, taking his outstretched hand, but he soon released hers, and slid his hand round her waist, and after a moment, almost as if shyly, to her breast. She felt her heart beating very fast. He squeezed and held her closer. She had looked out of the window at the shimmering sea and the people on the promenade, the traffic, the small boats close to the shore, but all of these things faded. She felt herself being turned towards him, felt the pressure of his hands, his body, his lips. He kissed her fiercely, far, far more passionately than before this day, and she felt herself responding, felt a great longing.

He carried her to the bed.

She had never dreamed that she could be so happy as she was when, afterwards, they lay side by side, with only a sheet over them, and his hand still warm upon her.

This, the second of May, was their wedding night.

Gideon chuckled at the antics of an American actor on the screen.

"Good tonight, isn't it?" he said.

"Shhhh!" hushed his youngest child.

Little Peter Wray slept on the folded blanket, the sheets of newspaper and the old mackintosh in a corner of the room, near the door of the cupboard, while his mother slept the sleep of the drunk on a single bed in the far corner. The greasy newspaper from which they had eaten the fish and chips was still on the table, and the warm day had brought out the flies, which were feasting.

Mrs. Crow, with a sister who tried to help her, sat pale-faced and dull-eyed in the front room of her house. From there she could see the roadway, and would know at once if anyone brought her child home.

The body of poor, suffocated Mr. Henderson, badly scarred, still lay on the morgue slab. Warr, now at home, was making notes and checking every detail of what he had done that day: he would work until the small hours if necessary, and his wife knew better than to disturb him. Mrs. Smallwood, the housekeeper who was under suspicion, was in a pub not far from the place where her employer had died, being treated to whisky after whisky by a pretty young girl and an attractive young man who represented a weekly newspaper which specialised in True Life Crime.

Quick Joe Mann sat at the front door of his daughter's house, in his shirtsleeves on this warm evening, and smiled amiably at a constable, who nodded as he passed by. Upstairs in the house, Joe's daughter had a handbag on her arm, while another woman practised the art of opening the handbag and stealing the contents.

When this lesson was over, the daughter called Joe in to his supper.

"When are you going to start the kids working again?" she wanted to know.

"I've been told to lay-off for a bit, too many been caught lately," Joe answered. "It won't be for long."

A bewildering variety of other things were happening in London, of course. The law which Gideon had to enforce was being broken in a thousand different ways by thousands of different people. Licensees of public houses and hotels were serving drinks after hours, usually with some apprehension; policemen were watching some of them suspiciously. Other police were making their rounds of the main streets, all brightly lit, where cars were parked, sometimes without lights; and those cars more than fifty yards from a street lamp were being noted, so that their owners could be charged for parking without lights even though no one could charge danger to the public. In back rooms behind the glittering signs of small clubs, gaming was going on, and the police were taking notes of the patrons, preparing reports for raids likely to be made during the next week or two. Here and there, dope was being sold in cigarettes, or injected with blunt hypodermic needles, but the police knew very few of the places where this was being done. On the railways and at big bus depots, petty pilfering was going on expertly, always with care and caution. One postman out of tens of thousands slipped a couple of fat registered envelopes into his pocket, and hoped that he would never be found out. Three illegal operations were being performed on young girls, each suffering agony which she believed was better than the shame and anguish of carrying a child. Thieves were watching their opportunities, most quite boldly, opening windows, opening doors, walking about houses while people slept upstairs, even helping themselves to food from the kitchen, or to a drink. A few fences were buying stolen goods so hot that they stung the fingers; within twenty-four hours, most of the goods would have changed hands three or four times, making it almost impossible for the police to find out where it had gone.

Two men threw themselves into the Thames, one to drown, one to be pulled out by the river police.

Flying Squad cars were on the move; the Divisions and the Yard night staff were kept fairly busy.

It was just a London night.

Most of London slept, but there was no sleep for Eve Dennis, in the small soundproof apartment in the heart of London. There was only terror because she believed that her husband was going to kill her.

There he was, in the doorway, with the knife.

She pushed the bedclothes back and got out of bed, and backed to the window. It was in the same wall as the kitchen window, but was much larger. Beyond was the blank wall of the building, and beneath the concrete alley. She could not go to the door because he was there, but the window was wide open on this warm night.

"Reggie," she breathed, "put that knife away and come to bed. Reggie! *Reggie!*"

5

SUICIDE?

LEMAITRE was alone in Gideon's office next morning, with the daily report ready, a thicker one than on Monday, but still not a record for side. Gideon's arrival brought a swift succession of telephone calls which Lemaitre answered one after the other, often with the smoke curling up from his cigarette into his eyes. Gideon noticed this more than he did usually; it reminded him of the days when Lemaitre had been a chain-smoker largely because of his domestic troubles.

That decree absolute, of course. Today?

Gideon did not allow himself to be distracted, but studied each report closely and made a note about officers whom he wanted to see. When he had finished, Lemaitre was enjoying a lull.

"'Morning, George."

"Hallo, Lem. They been making you work?"

"Willing horse, that's me. Four new things just come in, nothing very much, though. Madrid's okayed that extradition, Webster's bringing Riddall back with him, should be here tomorrow or the next day. Planes are all booked up. The Kent job's all over, we needn't send a chap down there after all – they've charged a middle-aged nightwatchman, looks pretty tight. Biggish burglary out at Stratford, van load of tobacco and cigarettes, but the Division can look after that, I should think. And hope! Suicide, according to first reports, over at Chilton Court"

"Suicide how?"

"Girl jumped out of a sixth-floor window. Broke her neck and cracked her skull. She wasn't found until this morning, when she was cold and stiff. Only been married a couple of weeks."

"Who's handling it?"

"Dick Sparrow."

"Well, no one will pull the wool over his eyes," Gideon remarked, and turned back to the reports. "Anything in about the Crow child?"

"Nope."

"Did you send that request to Divisions to check on the mothers of those kid thieves?"

"Yes, George," answered Lemaitre, with a mock humility which told Gideon that he was convinced the child crime-wave was over, and that Gideon was making too much of it.

Gideon made no comment, but for the next half-hour talked to men ranging from Superintendents to Sergeants, hearing comments, making suggestions, generally briefing them; and Lemaitre, who took notes and looked after the telephone, marvelled as he had always marvelled at Gideon's grasp of the details of each job. He made it look so easy. Four cases coming up in the magistrates' courts that morning needed special comment, but none was big enough to take Gideon out of the office. It looked as if he would be able to put everything really shipshape before the day was out.

Lemaitre went out for five minutes, and Gideon's telephone bell rang.

"Gideon . . . Oh, yes, Dick, how's it going? . . . Eh . . . well, I suppose I could look in for half an hour, I wouldn't mind a breath of air. Muggy this morning, isn't it? . . . What's on your mind?"

He listened, made one or two notes, studied them after ringing off, and then called Information.

47

"Anything at all in about the Crow child, or the father?"

"No, sir."

"See that I get a message just as soon as you hear something, will you?" Gideon rang off, scowled at the wall, and pictured Mrs. Crow, so haggard-looking, so despairing, so sure that her husband had stolen the child. Reports from all over the country made it certain that Crow and Sheila had not left since the first calls had gone out, but there was still the possibility that they had gone before anyone realised what Crow was up to.

For the first time, Gideon opened the batch of newspapers piled on his desk. Except for *The Times* and *The Guardian,* every one had printed a picture of Mrs. Crow, Sheila and the father. Gideon studied the father's face closely. He looked a younger man than Mrs. Crow, he was handsome in a way, had plenty of dark hair, and a rather wide parting which showed up white.

NATIONWIDE HUNT FOR MISSING CHILD

ran the headline in the *Globe,* and the others were much the same:

FATHER AND DAUGHTER VANISH.
GRIEF-STRICKEN MOTHER SAYS FIND MY CHILD.
YARD WATCHING ALL PORTS.

Here WAS the human appeal story, and here was Mrs. Crow's photograph.

Was Crow so clever that he had sneaked abroad?

Gideon telephoned CD Division.

There was an overtone of anxiety in Carter's dry, rather sardonic voice.

"I hope this beggar hasn't got away, George. He's not been to his office since Saturday."

"Been into his flat?"

"Oh, yes."

"Checked at nearby hotels, and the homes of his friends?"

"I tried to say in my report that I'd checked everything."

"Did Crow have any favourite holiday resort, anything like that?"

"Well—"

"Did he?"

"He was very fond of the New Forest, any forest for that matter. Loved trees."

"Ask Winchester to keep an eye open," said Gideon, and after a pause, went on: "How much do you know about Crow himself? The first reports said he was a hard drinker, pretty loose-liver, that kind of thing. Right?"

"Right-ish."

"Meaning?"

"Well, he played around a bit, but if I had to give an opinion, George, his wife was responsible for that. The cold type. Don't hold me to that, but the picture I'm getting is of a wife who wasn't very bed-willing, nagged a bit, felt she'd married beneath her. She probably saw herself as very hard done by, and may have caused most of the trouble herself."

"How about the girl Crow took home, then went off with?"

"They had a few weeks together, then he paid her off," Carter said. "He's been living in a service flat ever since."

"Emotional type?"

"What are you driving at, George?"

"I wouldn't like him to kill himself and the girl," said Gideon quietly. "Anything to suggest that he might?"

Carter said slowly: "I wouldn't think so, but there isn't much doubt that he missed the child very badly."

"How long's he been living on his own?"

"Twelve months or so."

"Seen his doctor?"

"No."

"Check with him, will you, see if there's any evidence of neurosis, extreme sleeplessness, anything which might help to turn his mind."

"All right, George."

"Thanks," said Gideon. He rang off, and dabbed his handkerchief over his forehead; it was not sunny today, but the office was much warmer than it had been yesterday. Lemaitre was back, and Gideon switched from the Crow child case to the suicide at Chilton Court. "I'm going over to have a word with Dick Sparrow, Lem, hold the fort, will you?"

"Yep. Anything special?"

"No. This suicide angle made me wonder if Crow could have decided to kill himself and the girl. Only an angle." Gideon, standing up, looked almost shamefaced. "Carter's checking." He knotted his blue tie and went out, passing half a dozen men on his way to the lift, noticing that all of them looked sweaty and warm. The last man he saw was the Detective-Sergeant cyclist whom he had passed last night. The man hesitated, then made as if to go past.

"'Morning, Arkwright," Gideon said. "Want me?"

"Well—not really, sir."

"What's on your mind?"

"Silly little thing, sir, really." Arkwright was young enough to feel that he might be making a fool of himself, and to colour slightly as he went on: "Seeing you last night jolted my memory about a chap I noticed yesterday morning, all dolled up and wearing a carnation in his button-hole as if he was going to a wedding."

"No crime." Gideon smiled.

"Last time I saw him, it was just after his wife had died. That Highgate food poisoning job. Remember it, sir?"

Gideon frowned. "I remember the job, yes. Six deaths, weren't there, and a newly married couple was involved? The husband came through, the wife died."

"Same chap, sir."

"Well, it's a decent interval."

"That's what I keep telling myself," said Arkwright, with a grin.

"Any Registry Office near there?"

"Cork Street."

"Oh. Well, he might have been best man or a guest, but if you're round that way you can look in and take a peek at the register, it might satisfy your curiosity," said Gideon. He nodded and walked on, only subconsciously aware of the fact that he had made a friend, and perhaps helped to shape a Detective who would train his powers of observation to their absolute limit. It was the man who noticed an odd feature of an everyday affair who really helped to prevent crime.

Gideon drove to Chilton Court, near the river.

He often passed these blocks of flats on his way to and from the office, and had never liked them. The blocks had been built just before the Second World War, when material had been cheap. The architect hadn't thought much about window space, while the landlord's one ambition had been to use every square foot of land. He had succeeded; there was the narrowest of drives approaching each block, and scarcely enough room in between the blocks. Two police cars were outside and one was just inside the driveway. A few idlers stood about, and two uniformed policemen. Gideon went to the entrance hall, and a constable said: "Mr. Gideon, sir?"

"Yes."

"Mr. Sparrow would be grateful if you'll go straight up, sir. Flat 69."

"Thanks."

The elevator was as small as it could be, self-operated, and with room only for four people. It crawled upwards. An advertisement announcing furnished and service flats for rent made a special point of the claim that the flats were all soundproofed.

A policeman was outside the open door of Number 69, and another was just inside. Several men were moving about in the two rooms beyond. These were small, too, and Gideon wondered how high the rent was. Then he saw Dick Sparrow, a man who looked rather like a bulldog, even to his snub nose and puckered lips. He was young for a Divisional Superintendent, in the middle forties, and was known to be one of the best raconteurs in the Force.

He came hurrying out of a small room on the right.

"Hallo, George, thanks for coming." He deliberately stopped Gideon from going right in, and drew him out into the passage. "I just thought I'd like to know what you thought when you'd had a dekko at the place yourself. The husband says that he went to bed at the same time as his wife, and when he woke up, she was missing. He thought she was in the bathroom, dozed off again, and didn't discover until about half-past eight that the bedroom window was wide open. Says he looked out and saw her down there. But there's a queer thing."

"What?"

"Her footprints," Sparrow said. "Look."

There had been time for photographs. A Sergeant from the photography department was standing by, with several damp prints in a blotting-paper folder, while the foot-prints on the floor beneath the bedroom window and on a three-inch ledge at the window itself, were marked off in chalk and protected by a little bridge of plywood, to make sure that they could not be smeared. Knowing that Sparrow was hoping he had spotted something which his superior would miss, Gideon seemed to take a long time coming to a decision, although he believed that he had noticed that "something" very quickly. Sparrow and the photographer were looking at him almost eagerly. A man from Fingerprints came into the room, saw the trio, stopped and almost held his breath.

"She climbed out backwards," Gideon said, keeping a straight face.

Sparrow's expression was almost comical. The photographer threw up his hands.

"I told you so," said the Fingerprints man.

"She walked to the window backwards, too," went on Gideon.

"That's right," said Sparrow, "and if you're going to throw yourself out of the window, would you walk backwards? How about the prints in the kitchen?" he asked the man from

Fingerprints.

"Can't be sure, she wasn't bare-footed in there," he was answered, "but I did pick up something."

"What?"

"The backs of a pair of shoes were scraped against the wall beneath the window in the kitchen," said the other. "It's a bit damp, and slightly powdery. I'd say she had been standing with her back to that window quite a lot."

"Think someone scared her into backing to the window and jumping out, do you?" Gideon said. "It's going to be a hell of a thing to establish." His voice was soft. "Sent the body away?"

"Yes," Sparrow answered. "Fractured skull and broken neck, death was instantaneous. No signs of bruises except where she fell. Clinton's doing the P.M. but Jameson and I had a good look at her, and the only visible injuries were from that fall. Of course if we could find anything in the stomach—"

"Where's the husband?"

"Downstairs with a neighbour."

"How is he?"

"He'd like us to believe he's hardly capable of making a statement." Sparrow raised a finger, and a plainclothes man who had been in the doorway came hurrying. "Let's hear Dennis's statement, Jim, will you?"

The shorthand note-taker did not even have to turn over the pages, he was so well prepared. The statement was brief and coherent; in fact a model, almost the kind of statement that a man advised by counsel would make. Dennis had woken up, noticed that his wife was missing from her bed, thought she had gone to the bathroom, woken again half an hour later, about half-past eight but he wasn't sure of the time, had noticed the open window, looked out, and seen her. He rushed down to make sure it was his wife, telephoned for a doctor, then gone downstairs. The doctor had arrived within ten minutes.

"How'd he tell you all this?" Gideon asked.

"In bits and pieces," Sparrow said. "When I read it over I

noticed that it was pretty smooth."

"Neighbours?"

"After he'd phoned the doctor, he told the people in a third-floor flat – the people he's with now – that she'd been queer since he married her, but he hadn't noticed it before. Says she had a kind of fear of crowds and people, and wouldn't go out. That squares with other statements I've had taken, George – he often went out, but she seldom did, especially this past few days. He did the shopping, too, grocery store, butcher's and all that kind of thing. Funny kind of start to married life."

"What's his job?"

"Radio salesman, but he says he came up on the pools last year, and has all he needs to live on for a while."

"Tell you what," said Gideon, "I'll give him the once over, but won't say much to him. If I play the strong silent copper, it won't help his nerves if he's got anything on his conscience. Then you keep plugging away with questions about his wife's behaviour, and did she see a doctor, did anyone else notice she was odd? Press him hard, but don't even whisper that she climbed out backwards. Have all the neighbours questioned, find out more about his background and the wife's, see if there's a history of mental instability. Call me or Lemaitre if you want extra help. Get everything done quick, so that he can't get his second wind."

Sparrow and the others were smiling, as if with a kind of relief.

"Fine," said Sparrow. "Thanks."

Ten minutes later, Gideon saw Reginald Dennis, widower of the dead Eve. Dennis was one of the neutrals, and Gideon felt no emotional reaction. He was pleasant-looking, dressed quite well, spoke with a slightly exaggerated "Oxford" accent, the type likely to impress a girl who did not know a great deal about men. He was still agitated, but his eyes had a kind of calmness, and Gideon could well understand why Sparrow had begun to wonder exactly what he knew.

Gideon was hard-voiced and forbidding.

"Most regrettable circumstances, Mr. Dennis. Be good enough to give Superintendent Sparrow all possible information. Important that all the causes of the tragedy should be found out quickly. Very quickly." He nodded curtly and turned away, with a suspicion that Dennis's eyes were not quite so calm when he finished as they had been when he had begun.

He could leave this to Sparrow quite safely now, all Sparrow had wanted was permission to go ahead. The fingerprint man and photographer were good, the fingerprint man especially; noticing those marks beneath the kitchen window and those on the shoes was first class. A man to watch. Gideon made a mental note of them both as he went down in the slow lift, which seemed even smaller than when he had come up. He wasn't surprised that three newspapermen were outside, had a word with them, assured them blandly that he was just doing his rounds, as usual, the case had all the hallmarks of a suicide, and went almost as blandly to his car. He flicked on the radio when he was round the corner, called Lemaitre, and asked: "Anything fresh in, Lem?"

"Nothing to worry about."

"I'll be around the West End if I'm wanted."

"Okay," said Lemaitre.

Gideon drove to Whitehall, left his car where the general public could not park, and then began to walk round London's Square Mile. Here, near Piccadilly, in Soho, and around Leicester Square, was the beat he'd trodden as a flattie, the manor he'd worked in as a Chief Inspector, the part of London which seemed closer to him than any other. His battles with Frisky Lee had been centred about here, for Frisky had once owned several second-hand jewellers' shops, where stolen goods had been on sale. Two managers had been trapped and one was still in jail; but neither had implicated Frisky.

No one ever did, because he frightened them into silence.

Gideon felt quite sure of that, and it was the real reason for his hatred of the man. As he walked the familiar hard pavements, he came to a sudden decision. Things were fairly slack at the Yard, and he could use a few days away, to think clearly and refresh his mind.

"I'll take a few days off with Kate," he decided, and then saw a policeman whose face was familiar. It was William Smith, who had been in Hyde Park on Sunday, and had spoken to the woman who had struck the child. The man was walking his week-day beat, in Regent Street, and raised his hand in salute.

Gideon stopped.

"Hallo, Smith. Did you check with the other chaps about that woman and the boy?"

"Yes, sir."

"Any results?"

"Two of them have seen her give the child a hefty slap for no reason at all, but that's as far as I've been able to get, sir," said Smith. "She's only in the park on Sundays. No one's seen her or the boy acting suspiciously. One of the fellows saw her dragging the boy along Oxford Street pretty roughly, though."

"Do you know her name?"

"No, sir."

"All right, but if you see her again, point her out to one of our plainclothes chaps, and ask him to find out where she lives and anything else he can about her. He can let me know."

"Very good, sir." Smith was obviously gratified.

"Right," said Gideon. "'Morning." He went on, walking more briskly, reached his car and drove straight to the Yard. He noticed that Warr's car was there, and Warr seldom came back from a job during the day unless he had something heavy on his mind, or had finished a job. Had he charged old Henderson's housekeeper? That wouldn't be surprising.

Lemaitre was alone in the office, looking greasy and hot, his collar undone and tie hanging down, a burn-blackened cigarette in the corner of his mouth. He was glancing through a newspaper; Gideon suspected that it had been at the back page and the racing reports until he heard footsteps.

"How'd it go?" asked Lemaitre.

"Sparrow's got a notion that the girl might have been pushed. If he wants any special help, see he gets it quick," said Gideon. "Anything else in?"

"Warr's back, looking as if someone's stolen the Sunday School Treat fund," Lemaitre said. "I said I'd tell him the moment you got in. Okay?"

"Okay," said Gideon.

6

NEED FOR PATIENCE

OBVIOUSLY Warr had a lot on his mind. He came in more quickly than usual, and without opening the door and leaving it ajar as if eavesdropping. Although his clerical grey suit was thick, and made him look plumper than he was, he did not seem to be too hot. There was an unusual air of briskness about him, and his smile was quite bright, too.

"Sit down, Syd," Gideon greeted. "Sorry I kept you."

"Hardly had time to get all my notes finished," Warr said. "George, I think I was wrong about Mrs. Martha Smallwood."

"Think she killed Henderson ?"

"It certainly wouldn't surprise me," Warr said. "I think you're going to hate my guts before I've finished."

"Try me."

"I want three if not four exhumations."

Lemaitre, at his desk and now studying reports, started to exclaim, then choked the sound back; neither of the others turned round. Gideon's expression was almost solemn.

"Let's have the rest, Syd."

"I spent an hour this morning looking through some of the old files of elderly gents who died mysteriously, and there was a *Globe* picture of a man up in Scarborough who died suddenly from gastro-enteritis, according to the doctor's certificate,"

Warr said. "Scarborough sent it down for our opinion. Well, the old gent had a housekeeper. Her picture was there, too. She was Martha Smallwood, Henderson's housekeeper. So the first thing I did this morning was to check with her friends where she'd worked before. She hadn't told all of 'em, but there's no doubt she's been in Bournemouth, Eastbourne and Weymouth during the past four years. Remember these jobs?" He took a folded envelope from his pocket, extracted a sheet of paper and handed this to Gideon. "Not exactly identical, but with some common features, George. The Bournemouth man died in a fire – the way Henderson was supposed to have died. The Weymouth man was hale and hearty. Died in his bath, though; heart attack, and he slumped down and was drowned. The Eastbourne man fell down the stairs and broke his neck. I've telephoned to all three places, and the housekeeper in each case answer's Martha Smallwood's description."

Now that he had played his cards, Warr sat back with a satisfied, almost smug smile.

"Think I'll get those exhumation orders, George?"

"Nice work," Gideon said, "although I can't say I'm looking forward to it. It means getting the Old Man to contact all the Chief Constables, and we'll strangle ourselves in red tape if we're not careful. Now you've started it, how would you like to see it all through?"

"Starting where?" asked Warr.

"Go and tell the Old Man about it all, lay everything on the table, suggest that we ought to keep it very quiet for a few days, if we can, and that I advise you to go down to Bournemouth, Eastbourne and Weymouth, and have a talk with the people on the spot. It'll take a week. We can have Mrs. Smallwood watched, although once Henderson's buried she won't think that she's got anything to worry about. How does it sound?"

"George," said Warr, taking a deep breath, "I always knew you were the best man for your job. Give me an hour, and I'll ask the Old Man to see me. And thanks a lot."

He went out, closing the door very softly, as if anxious to

overhear anything that was said as he disappeared. Lemaitre waited until the door was firmly closed, then grinned across and said: "You get 'em all eating out of your hand, I don't know how you do it."

"Warr hasn't had a break for a long time, and he's earned this one," Gideon said. "It'll give the Press a holiday and we'll be up to our necks. Think you could keep your end up here if I took two or three days off?"

"Damn sure I could," said Lemaitre. "Glad to know you've got some sense, a few days' holiday before you're run off your feet is just what you need. Good time for it, too. Take a tip from me, George."

Gideon smiled.

"Always ready for advice."

"Go away from London," Lemaitre said. "Take Kate away with you. Let the kids look after themselves for a day or two, it won't do them any harm."

"Something in that," agreed Gideon.

"There's a lot in it," Lemaitre said, "and you couldn't have chosen a better time for me, George. I had a call from my solicitor while you were out. The decree absolute's okay, she's free to marry the so-and-so, and I'm as free as the air. In case you haven't noticed it, I've been a bit on edge this last few days, and I wouldn't mind sticking my nose into more work than usual. I'm all right, though. I'm cured. And when you're back, I'll take a few days off among the Brighton breezes. It'll be like turning back twenty years. Like to hear my wolf whistle?"

Gideon chuckled, and said: "The look in your eyes is enough."

It took Kate five minutes to make up her mind.

"It'll be wonderful!" she said.

Gideon had an almost guilty feeling when he left the Yard in the middle of the afternoon. He'd spent an hour with Lemaitre, going over everything pending; had talked to the Assistant Commissioner for Crime about outstanding cases of importance, and particularly about Warr and his discovery; Warr had been given *carte blanche,* and the local police had been asked to give him all the assistance he needed. His greatest worries were the missing Crows, father and daughter, and the young wife who had crashed to her death at Chilton Court, walking backwards to the window, then "falling" out. Before leaving the Yard, he had talked to the chief pathologist, Dr. Clinton, and been assured that all the injuries had been caused by the fall, that there was no poison, nothing in the body to suggest that Mrs. Dennis had died from any cause but the fall. Sparrow was digging very deep, and it was already known that the girl died worth about seven thousand pounds, inherited from her mother three years ago. She had known Dennis three months before getting married.

Sparrow wasn't going to find it easy to build up a case against the husband.

Gideon was uneasy, too, about the missing father and daughter, the Crows. No word had come from the New Forest, and such a complete disappearance was unusual. But Brighton made it easy to forget.

"George," Kate said, on the second afternoon, "I'm not going to bathe alone. You come in."

"We don't want a tidal wave," Gideon objected placidly.

"The truth is, you've forgotten how to swim."

"Oh, have I?" said Gideon, because she was so obviously anxious for him to bathe. So he went across to the hotel, changed, and joined her again on the beach. The sting of the water made him regret it at first, but he was soon kicking out and fooling.

He bought an evening paper at the porter's desk, while Kate ordered tea on the bedroom balcony; that way, they needn't change until dinner. He sat glancing through the paper, the sun hot on the matt of greying hair on his chest, and then suddenly stiffened.

"Now what have you seen?" Kate demanded, taking off her cap and shaking her hair loose. "I refuse to let you cut this holiday short."

"No need for that," Gideon assured her. "Two more children were caught shop-lifting in Oxford Street yesterday, though, one nine, one ten years old."

"Taught by their mothers?" asked Kate.

"Don't know yet, but it looks all part of a pattern," Gideon answered. "That business is getting right under my skin. Remember the boy I told you about on Sunday?"

"The one whose mother hit him?"

"If it was the mother. We haven't traced 'em yet," Gideon told her. "Daresay we could if we went all out, but – oh, well. Can't find out where these mothers learn the job, either – the thing ought to be like ABC, and instead we're up against a brick wall. What worries me is how far it might spread." There was a tap on the door. "There's the tea, anyway, that might get the salt water out of my mouth."

Kate grimaced at him.

That was the moment, although Gideon never knew it, when Robert Carne saw and recognised him.

Marion looked really something in a bathing suit, a one-piece which for her was a little daring, but nothing like that seemed to matter when she was with Robert. The happiness which had caught her in a stranglehold within a few hours of the marriage seemed to grow and grow. He was so gentle, so understanding, obviously so full of love, and so happy himself. They swam a lot, sailed a little in the hired yachts from the beach, went to a show every night, after two or three hours in their room between tea-time and dinner; unbelievable hours to Marion. She felt that Robert was so completely hers that their life together could not fail to be an idyll. She thought of children. She wondered if she would conceive quickly. She hadn't yet talked to Robert about a family, but there was plenty of time for that. She knew only that she was ecstatically happy, and that the very look of Robert whenever she saw him was enough to make her heart beat faster. Now and again she would see him walking along the promenade, when he had been out to buy a newspaper. Or she would see him wading out of the sea, water streaming from his body as he laughed and waved to her. There was no joy so great as the moment, after waking, when she turned to see him lying close to her, handsome, strong, tanned.

On the Thursday morning, it was a little cooler than it had been, although still sunny and bright. They decided to sail, not to swim, and spent two hours on the Channel, where there was hardly a ripple, then made for the shore. It was after they had helped the old boatman to haul up the little boat that Marion saw the change come over Robert.

She had gone ahead, to get off the big shingle which was the one drawback on the beach, and watched Robert as he paid off the boatman, then turned to follow her. He wore a pair of light grey flannels and a pair of white canvas shoes, that was all.

He seemed to stumble.

She thought he had stubbed his toe on a larger stone than usual, but he didn't look down, just stood absolutely still for two or three seconds, staring at a hotel across the promenade. She could see the way his lips tightened and his eyes narrowed, and she actually noticed how he clenched his hands by his side.

Then, abruptly, he turned towards her, and came on. She had a funny idea that he was hurrying, as if anxious to get away. When he joined her on the lower promenade, he nodded but didn't smile: the first time he had failed to greet her as if she was the only girl in the world.

"Robert, what's the matter?"

His eyes glittered, and he said abruptly: "Nothing's the matter, what are you talking about?"

"But, Robert—"

"I said nothing's the matter, didn't I? Let's get back to the hotel, I want a drink."

Silently, they went back.

Gideon had looked straight at him from the balcony; and Gideon represented all the police in England to Robert Carne, *alias* Roger Clayton.

Carne did not know that the sun had been in Gideon's eyes, and to him Carne had been just another man walking up from the beach.

"All right, sweetheart," Carne said, after lunch. "I agree that I did snap your head off, and I'm terribly sorry." He was standing close to Marion, holding her lightly and in such a way that she had to hold her head back in order to see him properly. "As a matter of fact, I saw a man who once cheated me of a small fortune. I thought I'd got over it, but when I saw him sitting on that balcony, having a holiday with *my* money—"

"Oh, darling, why didn't you tell me before? I'd no idea!"

"Well, as I told you, I thought I was over it, I don't like bearing a grudge. It was a business deal, and he cheated me. I'd be a lot better off today, but for him. But let's forget it." He kissed her gently. "I love you, understand?" He kissed her a little more passionately, and held her very close. "Never mind him, never mind anyone else in the world, let's worry about just you and me."

His teeth hurt her lips when he kissed . . .

"Darling," he said lazily, half an hour afterwards, "I hope you won't think I'm being stubborn, but since I saw Lister"—he had given the imaginary business rogue the name of Lister—"I can't keep my mind off business and money and that kind of thing. I told you all about how I'm fixed, didn't I? I've plenty of money coming in a few years' time, but it's on trust, and I only get the interest."

"That doesn't matter, darling."

"It does and it doesn't," said Carne, and looked straight into her clear, worshipping blue eyes. For a few minutes when he had seen Gideon he had felt dreadful, but it had not taken him long to recover, and the little brush with Marion had enabled him to talk to her about a subject he was anxious to discuss.

"It matters in several ways," Carne went on, and began to play with a few tendrils of her hair. "If I could use the capital, it would make things much easier. I could start my own business, and work from home. As it is, I'll have to start travelling as soon as we get home, and—well, I can't pretend I'm as enthusiastic as I was."

Marion looked at him steadily, and then asked: "How much will you be away, darling?"

"Well, it depends."

"What does it depend on?"

"The firm," said Carne, with a grimace. He sat up, pushed the pillows more comfortably behind him, and stretched out for cigarettes. "Comfy? You look wonderful!" His hand was firm upon her for a moment, and then he lit a cigarette; she did not smoke. "They might send me somewhere in the north or even Scotland or Northern Ireland, and I'd be away for three or four weeks. But that probably won't be for a month or so—"

Marion struggled up on her pillows.

"Three or four weeks!"

"Horrible, isn't it?"

"But, darling, I couldn't bear it, I just couldn't stand being separated for three or four *weeks.*" She made it sound as if it was a lifetime, and her expression of dismay was so comical that Carne had to laugh. "Darling, it's not funny, it's awful. I thought you might be away for two or three days at a time, but not weeks."

"When you work for a firm, you have to do what you're told," said Carne. "You know that, sweetheart. The trouble is that I've only the one qualification – I can *sell.* And I get larger commissions if I'm away longer, and better allowances, so in the long run it wouldn't be too bad, and I could probably get together enough cash to start a business which I could run from home. So I shouldn't worry too much. The boss isn't too bad, and he knows I've just got married. He'll probably agree that I can cover the Home Counties for the first few weeks, and that would mean I'd be home for week-ends."

"Week-ends," Marion echoed forlornly.

Carne blew cigarette smoke towards the sunlit window, and

then leaned over her and kissed her forehead.

"You'll soon be glad enough to get rid of me for a few days."

"Robert, don't say that."

"Well, you will."

"I'd hate it if you were away for one night."

"Hang it, sweetheart, I have to earn a living," he remonstrated. "After all, I've more responsibilities now, I have two to keep instead of one. And if we go on as we've started, we'll probably soon have a third!" He kissed her again, and stubbed out the cigarette. "Do you know what time it is?"

"It's about four. Darling, I didn't dream that you'd be away for long periods like that."

"But, sweet, I did tell you that I was a commercial traveller – or, if you prefer it, a travelling representative – and that I sell motor accessories which show a whale of a big profit. That's why I don't want to change the job for anything else, unless I set up in business for myself. But as that's not possible, it's no use talking about it. Darling—"

He broke off.

Marion had pushed the sheet back.

He bent over her, very slowly, and he said in a low-pitched, grating voice: "You think it's going to be hard on you when I'm away. How do you think I'm going to like it? Marion, you're beautiful, everything about you is beautiful . . ."

Unless he had completely misjudged her, it would not be long before she wanted to know what kind of business he would set up for himself, and how much money it would need. He was already determined on what he would say: as a wholesaler, of course, employing his own salesmen, and he would need about five or six thousand pounds, to buy stock, to pay salaries, rent and other expenses. It would be in his present business, and since they had first met, he had made sure that she knew how profitable that could be. He felt quite certain that before the week was out they would be planning the whole thing together, within two weeks he would have at least five thousand of her money. If he could squeeze it up to ten, that would be enough. The process should take about a month, and experience had told him that one month with any woman, even much prettier women than Marion, was as long as he could bear patiently. Once the newness wore off, there was no attraction for him.

As he watched her dressing, he wondered how much money she really had. It might be as well to find out before he started the "business". If she had much more than ten thousand, and willed it to him, or died intestate with him as next of kin, it might get him out of financial worries for the rest of his life.

As he dressed, he remembered how this subject had arisen, and wondered what risk there was of seeing Gideon of the Yard again. The wise thing would be to get away from Brighton proper, perhaps have a run in the country, or else spend the next day at Hove. Marion wouldn't mind. Marion would do anything for him.

Anything.

He did not see Gideon at the hotel or on the beach again.

"Robert," said Marion, on the Saturday afternoon.

"Yes, my sweet!"

"How much would it cost to start that business?"

"Oh, forget it, darling, I'm not going to start sponging on you."

"No, tell me."

"Well — if it's going to be done properly, it will cost about ten thousand pounds. It might be possible to launch it with half that, but I couldn't carry enough stock, and that's always a bad way to begin. Not that we need worry about it, I'm not even going to consider it."

"Darling," Marion said.

"Yep!"

"Don't be cross, but I simply can't bear the thought of you being away for days on end, and as for weeks—"

"Listen, Marion, it's my job. What's the use of arguing about it?" Carne was sharper than he had been with her before except after that one moment when he had seen Gideon. "There isn't anything to discuss."

"Well, I think there is."

"Marion, once and for all will you stop worrying about it? I'll look round for a job that will keep me nearer home and—"

"I don't want you to start looking round for jobs," Marion said, and her voice sharpened, too. "And there's no need to be so stubborn."

"Stubborn! I'd like to know who's being stubborn. You keep harping on the subject."

"And I shall, until you see sense."

"Marion, I am not going to sponge—"

"But if we start this business as equal partners, it won't be sponging," said Marion. "If a married couple can't be partners in a business, I'd like to know who can."

"Listen, Marion." Carne stood in front of her, by the window of the bedroom, in the gloaming of the Saturday evening. He held her hands tightly, and looked boldly into her eyes. In its way, it was the most convincing performance he had ever put on in all his vicious life. "Once money gets between us, we can be in trouble. If I could put up half, even a third, of the capital, it would be different. But I can't, for several years. If the business should fail—"

"But you know it inside out, it wouldn't fail!"

"Changes of circumstances, market conditions, anything like that could force the company into bankruptcy," Carne insisted. "And if I'd ruined you as well as myself, what kind of opinion do you think I'd have of myself? I've got to have some pride. For goodness' sake, why don't you see it my way?"

"Bob, it's no use," said Marion very firmly, "and I can see what's worrying you now. Well, even if the worst came to the worst and we lost every penny – which we won't – it wouldn't ruin me, or anything like it. I've at least three times the money we'd need."

Carne kept a straight face; no gleam showed even in his eyes, and the pressure of his fingers on hers was no slighter. He stood quite still for what seemed a long time, while Marion searched his face for some indication of his reaction; he knew that she was worrying in case she had upset him.

It was hard not to laugh.

"Look, darling, let's forget it for this evening," he said more gently. "That does make a difference, but it doesn't alter the principle of the thing. Perhaps we can work out some legal way in which you have a share of the trust money, when it falls due. But let's forget it tonight."

"All right, sweet," Marion said.

Her eyes told him that she was sure that she had won.

Won!

She lay asleep.

He was by the window, looking out on to the calm, moonlit sea, seeing a few couples walking along the promenade, but making no sound.

He kept saying the same thing to himself over and over again.

"Thirty thousand pounds, that would see me right for the rest of my life."

7

THE SECOND SUNDAY

ABOUT half-past three on that Saturday afternoon, Gideon turned his car into the street in Hurlingham where he lived, and slowed down. It was a wide street of Victorian houses, solid-looking, well-kept and well-painted. Gideon's was among the most attractive; he took great pride in this house, into which he and Kate had moved when they had first married, and where all their children had been born.

Kate was tanned, her eyes were clear, she looked contented.

"Here we are, then," Gideon said. "I wonder if any of the young 'uns are in to greet us."

"I told them they needn't be," Kate said. "Matthew will be playing cricket, Pru's got an evening concert, and Penelope isn't often home on Saturday afternoons these days." She got out of the car, and led the way to the front door.

The narrow hall was shiny and bright, there was no trace of dust. On a small table was a bowl of daffodils, large and beautiful, trumpeting a silent welcome towards the homecomers. Without a word, Kate looked into the front room; there were daffodils and early tulips. She shot a glad, almost girlish glance at Gideon, and they went along to the kitchen.

"Bless their hearts," she said, "they've got it looking like a new pin. I wonder where—"

A sudden burst of giggling interrupted her, from behind the kitchen door. That was fourteen-year-old Penelope, who couldn't keep quiet any longer. Then Prudence and Priscilla, who were eighteen, came bursting upon them, happy in their surprise, and seventeen-year-old Matthew stood grinning, too, obviously righteous in the knowledge that he had done his share. The kitchen-cum-dining-room was as bright and spotless as the other rooms, the big table was laid for high tea, and a kettle was singing.

That night, Gideon spent over an hour looking at television, to finish off his holiday. That had helped in two ways. He was quite sure that his desire to stop Frisky Lee from leaving the country was because of his absolute belief that Frisky had been fooling the police for years, and was now cashing in on that; he was equally sure that the child thieves stemmed from the same central source, which must be traced. Any woman who could train her own child to thievery was far, far worse than a whore.

That night, Peter Wray was at the cinema. It was one of his good nights, one of the highlights of existence. He often went on Saturday night, usually to a different theatre for three or four weeks, so that he was not at the same place too often. He knew nothing about the reasons for that. He did not even think that it would be nice if he could sometimes choose the film he would like best. A U film or an A film, they were all the same, except that if it was an A, his mother took him through the paybox and lost him in the cinema itself.

He knew exactly what he had to do.

She had taught him.

His fingers were as dexterous as a child's fingers could be, and no one in London had a lighter touch. His mother had pointed out the bulging pockets which contained wallets, the handbags which could be opened easily in a crowd, the trick of taking out the contents and putting a wallet back so that the victim had no idea how the money had been lost. He knew the kind of thing his mother liked best, and that it must be paper money or small jewels; no silver, because silver made a noise. He was always taken in a little while before the last house, so that he could come out and mingle with the pushing crowds, some trying to get in, some coming out; there was usually a crush, and most Saturday nights he picked seven or eight pockets, or seven or eight handbags.

He had never yet been caught, but knew exactly what to do and say if he were to be, how to look piteous, how to apologise. He knew it was wrong in the general sense, because he knew that he had to be wary of policemen and any kind of authority, but he also knew what his mother would do if he were caught, or if he had a bad night. Some nights at the pictures had been ruined because he had stolen so little, but in the past six months there had been nothing to worry about, he was so expert.

His small hands darted to and fro, to and fro.

He was in luck that night; the main film was a Western, and he saw nearly half of it before going into the crowded foyer. He had six successful pickings before the crowd thinned, and passed these spoils on to his mother, who was sitting at an end seat, ready to take them. Then he went back to his own seat and saw the whole programme through. It was a little after eleven o'clock when he returned to the dingy street and the tall, grey house. He went slowly up the wooden, creaky stairs. When he reached the top, he hesitated because he heard sounds, then his mother's voice, and a man's. He stood in a darkness relieved only by a crack of light at the side of the door, and it reminded him of the cupboard. He shivered. He knew what might happen if he went in, now, and after a while he turned away and went towards the window which overlooked the backs of houses. He was hungry and thirsty, but tired above all, and he lay down on the bare dusty boards, shifted his position several times, tried to make his head comfortable by resting it on his hands, and then dropped off to sleep.

He did not wake when the man left.

He did not wake when his mother opened the door, next

morning, looked across at him, and then went over and stirred him with her foot. He started up, trained to wake at that touch, and there was a moment of fear in him.

"Come on, get up," she said, "we're going to the Lane this morning. Get a move on, there's some bread on the table."

There was a slice and a half of dry bread, and some cold, weak tea.

But it wasn't a bad morning at all.

Gideon sat for an hour that Sunday morning, immersed in various reports. Taken by and large, they weren't too bad, and certainly there was nothing that he would have done differently if he'd been here all last week. Sparrow hadn't got any further on the Dennis job. The inquest verdict had been that Mrs. Dennis had taken her own life while the state of her mind had been temporarily disturbed. The girl had died intestate, worth about seven thousand pounds, so Dennis was that much the richer.

"Dennis will slip up," Gideon mused hopefully.

There were two reports from Warr. The Weymouth exhumation had been arranged with little publicity, and the name of the man whose remains had been disinterred had not reached the Press. The Bournemouth name had been announced, and there had been quite a splash in the local newspaper, but Warr had chosen his time well, and there had not been much in the Saturday morning newspapers. The full reports weren't in yet, but Warr had sent a letter saying that the results were likely to be as he had expected. Somewhere in Harrow, Martha Smallwood was probably sitting and brooding and wondering what the Bournemouth exhumation meant, and knowing that if she tried flight, she would be giving the game away. If she was guilty, then her safest course was to sit tight. Warr had asked that her earlier movements be traced, and the Yard was at work on that.

During the week, the three men involved in the bank robbery had been detained and charged; they were under remand.

There was still no news of Sheila Crow and her father, but Mrs. Crow had telephoned three times. Reports from all over the country showed how intensive the search was.

There was a note from Lemaitre.

"Looks as if you're right again, George. Those two kids picked up for shop-lifting last week were taught by their mothers all right, although I doubt if we'll prove it. Both live over at QR. I've asked Woodrow to check closely, to see if they know the other mothers."

Mothers . . .

The telephone bell rang.

Gideon lifted the receiver promptly, shifted his big pipe, put the receiver to his ear, and said: "Gideon."

"That you, George?" Obviously the speaker, a man with a marked Cockney accent, hadn't heard him. It was Superintendent Hemmingway of the NE Division.

"Hemmy? Could this be news about Frisky Lee?"

"Yup. Busy?"

"What's your trouble?"

"Trouble is one word," Hemmingway said, and the very tone of his voice told Gideon that this was no ordinary call. "I think I want everyone you've got."

"Let's have it," Gideon said briskly.

"Frisky Lee won't be emigrating, after all," said Hemmingway. "He's had his throat cut."

Gideon did not answer at once. He was picturing Lee and recalling his own reactions, his own positive belief that Lee was still active and operating a dozen kinds of crime. If he was right, then whatever Lee had done could now be burst wide open. Here was a chance in a lifetime.

Yet the fact that Lee was dead caused a kind of disappointment, as if Lee had defeated him right to the end.

Crazy thought.

"All right, I'll be over," Gideon responded. "What do you want to do for a start?"

"I think we ought to have every mother's son of a fence

watched today," said Hemmingway. "That's as far as I've got."

"You're right, and I'll lay it on," promised Gideon. He jotted down one or two notes on a pad, then stretched out for another telephone. "See if you can get me Mr. Lemaitre, at his home," he said into this, and then to Hemmingway: "No, I wasn't speaking to you. When did it happen?"

"During the night."

"When was he found?"

"Half an hour ago. His wife found the body in the bedroom."

"Sleep together?"

"Posh, Frisky was. Separate rooms."

"Anyone in mind?"

"About two hundred and fifty people within a stone's throw of where I stand would have liked to see the end of Frisky," said Hemmingway, "and so far I don't know where to start. I've got my chaps over there, the place is cordoned off, although it's a hell of a job in the Lane on a Sunday morning, and this'll make it worse. All the boys will come in to the party, and the more there are the more trouble they'll make for us, so they'll have a wow of a time. If you ask me, they'll start rock 'n' roll and then we really will see something."

"Okay, Hemmy," Gideon said. "I'll send a couple of Squad cars over right away, and some uniformed branch men. We've got to keep that place clear, if necessary we'll clear the Lane."

"It'd cause a riot!"

"Well, we've had riots before," Gideon said dryly. "I'll be over soon." He banged down the receiver as the other telephone began to ring.

"Mr. Lemaitre, sir."

"Thanks . . . Lem, sorry to worry you this morning, but there's trouble over at Petticoat Lane. Frisky Lee's had his throat cut."

Lemaitre's comment was almost a scream. *"What's that?"*

"I'm going straight over. Hemmingway suggests that we have every fence tabbed, and he couldn't be more right. I think that every boy who's carrying hot stuff and waiting for the market to rise will try to unload the moment he hears that Frisky's dead. They'll offer at cut rates for ready money. If I've been on the ball with Frisky, we'll pick up a dozen or more of the bigger boys."

"Hundreds!" Lemaitre said explosively. "Put a call out for all the C.I.s and Sergeants who are off duty this morning," he urged. "I'll be over in twenty minutes."

"Thanks."

"Damned if I don't hope you've been right," Lemaitre said, and it was easy to imagine his grin as he rang off.

Gideon picked up the other telephone, with no outward show of haste, and when the operator answered, he said: "I'm going to NE Division, and I don't want messages sent on unless they're vital . . . Thanks. Now call Mr. Willis, and tell him I'd like two—no, three—cars standing by. I'll look in myself and tell him what it's all about."

"Yes, sir."

"Thanks," said Gideon. He stood up from the desk, and shrugged his big shoulders into his coat; it was much cooler this morning, and the sky was grey. He slipped his pipe into his pocket, freshly filled with sweet-smelling tobacco, then went out and down the stairs. He wanted to get himself into exactly the right frame of mind for Petticoat Lane, and everything that was going to happen now. If he was right about Frisky, this murder was the biggest thing that had happened in London's underworld for twenty years, and could uncover a stinking cesspool of crime.

He mustn't miss a trick; the importance of it, and the fact that he had waited so long for this chance, had a peculiarly tautening effect on him. He felt an unfamiliar pounding of his heart, and had a queer feeling, almost a presentiment, that Frisky Lee might fool him even in death.

He sat at the wheel, and drove swiftly after the Flying Squad cars.

8

THE LANE

THE streets of the City were hushed and deserted. At the Bank of England, with the bank's mass of granite standing like a stronghold on one corner, and the pillars of the Royal Exchange giving a touch of gracefulness, the only moving things were a solitary red bus, two small private cars, three cyclists and five pedestrians with cameras, one man dark-skinned. The narrow streets leading towards Shoreditch, Aldgate and the East End beyond were almost empty, and the tall buildings which housed so much of the world's business were shuttered and silent. Unexpectedly, a traffic light stopped Gideon, and a policeman lurked round the corner, as if determined to catch any motorist who was reckless even in this Sabbath desert of stone.

The lights changed.

The quietness did not, until Gideon turned slightly left beyond Aldgate Pump, which had served the people for centuries, and from which water still poured. Ahead lay Aldgate and Whitechapel. Ahead lay Petticoat Lane, where he was going. Near the tube station, more people were about, hawkers with their wares were calling in subdued tones, one or two shops were open, people hurried to and from the underground station, fruit sellers were putting the finishing touches to their barrows like artists slapping paint upon a canvas already gay.

Here were cars, cyclists by the dozen, pedestrians still cautious as they crossed the road. Every hundred yards the traffic thickened. More policemen than usual were on duty at the road junctions. Gideon saw the crowd thickening, almost as if they were converging on the gates of a football ground. Above the noise of the engines of the cars there was also a background of sound, the muted one of raised voices. Gideon went on until he saw a mass of blocked vehicles and hopeless confusion, three policemen talking to drivers of cars who sounded indignant, others turning back cyclists and walkers. There seemed to be a kind of chorus.

"Sorry, sir."

"Can't come this way this morning."

"Turn back, second on the right, then first right and right again."

"Sorry, sir."

"Sorry, sorry, sorry."

Gideon pulled in at the side of the road, then walked towards the nearest policeman, who was a link in a cordon across the road. The traffic was not in such confusion as at first appeared, the police were sorting it out, soothing annoyed drivers who knew that this was the easiest way to Petticoat Lane. Then came other questions.

"What's up?"

"Been an accident?"

"Lots of cops arahnd this morning, ain't there?"

Gideon smiled at the policeman, who frowned as if he knew he'd seen this man somewhere, but couldn't be sure where. Then his face cleared and he saluted.

"Good morning, sir!"

"'Morning," said Gideon. "You've got a job on."

"Had many a worse, sir."

"That's all right, then," said Gideon, and went on.

Although the crowd and the traffic were being kept away

from this end of Petticoat Lane, the far end and the approach streets were thronged with people, all on the move. Frisky Lee's house was some way off. To reach it, Gideon had to enter Petticoat Lane itself, and this end was sealed off tightly by the police, but only for a few yards – as far as the little narrow turning of Medd Alley. Beyond, Gideon saw the seething mass, and it was even more crowded at this end because of the press of people at the police barrier. Some were merely curious, some almost desperately anxious to find out what had happened, some probably hoping to crash the barrier and rush Medd Alley, to trample over all the area which might hold a clue to the killer.

For if anything was certain, it was that this was an underworld killing.

A Police Sergeant in uniform came hurrying round the corner of Medd Alley, almost bumped into Gideon, apologised, and said breathlessly: "Mr. Hemmingway's along there, sir." He pointed to the massed crowds further along the Lane. "Picked someone up, I think."

"Thanks. How far?"

"Corner of Medd Street, sir."

"Thanks." Gideon turned away from the narrow alley, the police cars blocking it, the policemen on duty, and went towards the cordon across Petticoat Lane. Two men made way for him. At first, it looked as if he would have to push through a solid phalanx of East-enders out on their Sunday morning hunt for bargains, but slowly the outer crust gave way. The crowd lining the barrier was four or five strong, and Gideon studied it closely, being half a head taller than most of the people there. He saw sallow faces, olive-skinned faces, Jewish faces, Arabs, negroes, pale-faced Cockneys, men, women and children, a heterogeneous mass of people from all over the world.

He saw more.

At least a dozen criminals were among the crowd close to the barrier, men who had been inside, and most of whom would soon be in dock and in jail again.

The death of Frisky Lee had lured them like a magnet.

Gideon saw them looking at him, some openly, most furtively. Tired men, jaded men, unshaven men, smart men, young men, old men. Bright and gay-looking young women, painted women, women with their hair in curlers, women fresh from a perm, women with little hats perched on their heads, or with scarves tied round them, women without a trace of make-up, tired women, worried women.

Worried women, and worried men who knew that the lid had blown off the East End cauldron. Gideon had no doubt that he had been right, that Lee had been the master, and these frightened people his puppets.

A man called out from the thick of the crowd close to the barrier: "What's up, Gee-Gee?"

There was a quick laugh; but most of the people only smiled uneasily, watching to see Gideon's reaction. He stood still and looked about him, almost unbelievably solid and block-like, and without a trace of a smile, he said: "I'm told Frisky Lee had a heart attack."

He walked on.

He heard the gust of laughter behind him, knew that in that moment he had done himself, as head of the Criminal Investigation Department, a lot of good. The East End loved the wag. The East End was ready to accept a policeman as a human being provided he didn't act too much like God Almighty. And among this crowd were many who were only on the fringe of the game, by marriage or blood relationship, and who would warm to him.

Any one of them, now or later, might talk; might sneak into a telephone booth and call him up, and say: "So-and-so did it," or: "Talk to So-and-so about Frisky, why don't you?"

At last Gideon was through the crowd by the barrier, and in Petticoat Lane as it was on most Sundays. Here were the stalls, here was the fruit, the meat, the fish, the furs, the clothes, the toys, the hucksters, the vendors of cheap chocolate and sweets.

Here were the men and women on the pavements and in the doorways of the shops, calling to everyone who passed by, offering great bargains at tremendous sacrifice, from television and radio to oranges from across the sea. Here were the little, husky, confidential men slipping fountain-pens out of their pockets, "giving 'em away", here were the masses of goods, all clearly marked with prices which would compel most shopkeepers to shut their doors. Most of it was honestly bought, Gideon knew; most of the goods were sold at cut prices, quick profits from small returns; but there was at least one chance in ten that the television set being offered at auction with a starting price of twenty pounds had been stolen during the past few weeks. A tall, thin-faced, shrill-voiced auctioneer was offering it.

"Twenty pounds I heard, who'll give me forty? What's the matter with you this morning, a seventeen-inch television sound in wind and limb, greatest value on the market at its full retail price, and what am I bid? Pin money! Twenty pounds I'm bid, but that's no use to man or beast. Take it away, Charlie, they're a lot of skinflints this morning. What's that, sir? Twenty-five pounds I'm bid. Mind you don't break the bank, sir, you've got the devil in you today. Twenty-five pounds I'm bid for a television set which is guaranteed to show you the lowest necklines in the B.B.C. or I.T.A., so how about it? Charley, it's no use, I can't sell that for under thirty. Twenty-five I'm bid—twenty-six I'm bid—twenty-seven I'm bid—"

Gideon passed on, still watched by these anxious people.

The helmets of several policemen showed up not far away, and a crowd was getting bigger around them. The people in the Lane itself were thick as peas. A group of Americans were marvelling, their cameras clicking, and a girl was saying: "Did you ever see anything like it, Elsa?"

"How about this for the Farmer's Market?"

There was a group of silent Indians, the men in Western dress, the women in saris of beautiful colours. There was a family of four, middle-aged parents, two well-dressed public

81

school or preparatory school types, quiet-voiced but marvelling, their eyes radiant.

Over the heads of the crowd, Gideon saw Hemmingway, an elderly man, running to fat, flabby of face and pale. Hemmingway was within a few months of retiring age, and something about the look of him suggested that he should have retired before, even on a lower pension. The NE Division took a lot out of a man.

Then Gideon saw the child of Hyde Park. There was no mistaking the pale, peaky face, the rounded eyes which were too shiny and bright, the dirty clothes, the wary look. Last Sunday in the crowd round the soap-box orators of Marble Arch, this Sunday among the crowd in Petticoat Lane. There was no doubt now, he'd come to steal. His mother wasn't in sight, and before Gideon could get near, the child was lost among a forest of trousered legs and short skirts and pale gossamer called nylon.

Hemmingway looked up, and saw Gideon. He beckoned, with his head. A ring of police, a dozen strong, kept back the crowd, which surged forward to get a closer look when Gideon was allowed through. Beyond them were the cries of the market, the pleading of the auctioneers, the bustle, the munching, the lounging, the sightseeing. And here were three Detectives from the Division, including Hemmingway, the ring of police, and a man lying on the ground, still as death, with another man bending over him.

Gideon recognised a Divisional Police Surgeon, Dobson. Dobson straightened up, and said to Hemmingway: "He's dead all right, better get an ambulance."

"Any outward sign of the cause?"

"No."

Hemmingway turned, half a head shorter than Gideon, a little aggressive because he wasn't feeling sure of himself. Hemmingway always raised his voice when he felt that he might be criticised.

"We missed him by two minutes, that's all."

"Who is he?"

"Ratsy Roden," Hemmingway said. "He worked for Lee, usually slept at Lee's house, but he wasn't there this morning, so I put a call out for him. He was sneaking out of a shop, and one of my chaps saw him and gave chase. He just folded up, like this."

"Oh," said Gideon, and looked down at the small body of Ratsy Roden. Some men had no luck at all. Ratsy had a name which had acted like a curse all his life, and a thin face with a receding chin, a pointed nose and a sloping forehead. Any way one looked at it, Ratsy was an apt name. Now he lay dead, perhaps of his own hand, perhaps murdered, perhaps of natural causes.

"He was afraid we were searching the shops," Hemmingway said. "It wouldn't surprise me if we found that he killed Lee."

"What shop did he come from?" Gideon asked.

"Near Tod Cowan's place." Hemmingway nodded to a small corner shop, outside which were two stalls filled with men's clothes, and with socks and braces, suspenders and ties. "We'd better have a look round. If you'd rather go to Frisky's house, I won't be long."

"I'll stay with you," Gideon said. He walked with Hemmingway towards the shop, where a little man with a hooked nose stood in his shirtsleeves, a tailor's measure round his neck, thinning hair standing on end, an almost scared look in his big eyes.

Just behind him was a big, fat woman who looked sixty, and garish with hair dyed an unnatural-looking auburn, the more incongruous because it was in curlers. She wore a gaily coloured dress with a pattern of huge flowers, and this was a little too tight for her, especially at the hips. She darted nervous glances from Tod Cowan, her husband, to the Police.

"Tod, tell the gentlemen," she urged.

"Already I have told them," Tod Cowan said, and spread his hands. "Could I turn Ratsy away, a poor boy I have known all my life?"

"You would never have been so cruel, Tod," his wife asserted,

JOHN CREASEY

and her brown eyes steadied, to challenge Gideon and Hemmingway.

"That's right," Tod hurried to confirm, "I could never have been so cruel." He patted his wife's hand.

Gideon left this to Hemmingway, who might be aggressive because he expected blame for letting this go wrong, but was far and away the best man for dealing with the people of the East End. He was known to be fair, known to try and make sure that no one had a raw deal. He didn't smile, but asked mildly: "When did Roden come?"

"About six o'clock."

"Six o'clock it was," echoed Mrs. Cowan.

"Wake you up?"

"Yeth, he tapped at the window, Mr. Hemmingway. Frightened the life out of me, he did."

"Did he say why he'd come?"

"He said Frisky had been at him again, Mr. Hemmingway, that's what he told me," Cowan declared, and his wife nodded so vigorously that the dyed hair bobbed up and down in its tight wire curlers. "I didn't think that he'd done anything wrong," Tod added, "but even if I had, how could I say no to him? He was a good boy at heart, I know he was a good boy."

"Is that all he said?"

"On my heart, Mr. Hemmingway, he didn't say another word. I told him to make himself a cup of char and he slept in the corner of the shop, like he often does. When Frisky's in drink he's *terrible,* Mr. Hemmingway."

"He's a devil, that's what he is," damned Mrs. Cowan.

"What made Roden leave?" asked Hemmingway.

"Well, I was out here serving, and a policeman asked me a few questions, and I suppose Ratsy thought I'd mention him. All I know is that Ratsy came running out. I've never been so astonished in my life, Mr. Hemmingway, never indeed. He looked as if he was dying on his feet, he did really."

"All right, thanks," said Hemmingway. "You'll make a formal statement later and sign it, Tod, won't you?"

84

"Anything you say, Mr. Hemmingway."

"Anything at *all.*" The hair-curlers danced.

"Good. Now we'll have a look round the shop," said Hemmingway. "You can go upstairs to your living-room, Mrs. Cowan. And you, Tod."

He led the way inside as an ambulance bell sounded nearby, loud as if all London was sick. The police began to clear a path for it, and the Divisional Surgeon and the other Detectives stayed near the body.

Inside the outfitter's shop it was gloomy, for the windows were covered with huge signs, like BARGAIN—FINAL OFFER, and with huge painted prices. The walls were lined with racks of clothes, except at one side, where there was a long counter, with cabinets for shirts, socks, ties, the smaller items, behind it. In a corner was a dilapidated armchair of the type which could be let down to make a couch. By the side of this was an old overcoat, which had obviously been used as a blanket.

Hemmingway picked this up, and began to go through the pockets. Suddenly he snatched his hand away as if he had been stung.

"What is it?" Gideon demanded.

"It's a knife," Hemmingway said, and carefully turned the coat upside down and shook it, until a long, daggerlike knife slid out and fell on to the bed. The blade was coated with a browny kind of stain, except in one spot, which had been cleaned; and that spot glistened like silver.

"Did he do it, or was it planted on him?" Hemmingway asked.

"That's the question," said Gideon heavily. "I wonder how soon we'll know how Ratsy died."

9

FACTS ABOUT FRISKY

GIDEON felt the tensions crowding him as he stepped over the threshold: he would never have believed how tight a hold Frisky had on him; how deep and bitter was his resentment that the man had been able to hold him at bay.

Who had killed him, just three weeks before leaving for Australia with his lovely young wife and their child? Was the timing significant?

With luck, the wife would be in a state of emotional panic now; shocked, defenceless, alone. Soon a doctor would come hurrying and order the police not to question her; and Gabriel Lyon, Frisky's lawyer, would come, smiling and suave, to look after her interests as expertly as any man in London.

Gideon had to act fast.

The hallway was narrow in this three-storeyed house in a small terrace. Gideon had noticed that this one and its two neighbours had been freshly painted outside; inside, the hall was spick and span, and on a hall-stand was a jug of daffodils. It reminded him of his and Kate's homecoming, the day before.

Then, he heard a baby cry.

The sound came clearly for a second or two, then fell away into a gurgling, and into silence.

"Frisky's son," Hemmingway remarked.

86

"How's his wife?"

"Struck dumb," said Hemmingway.

"Genuine?"

"It looked like it," said Hemmingway. "We'll soon find out." A plainclothes Divisional man was at the foot of a narrow flight of stairs, and Hemmingway approached him, while Gideon realised that there was something a little odd about the look of the hall by the staircase and, stepping forward, saw that an archway had been made in the wall on either side. Glancing right and left, he saw other staircases; so three houses had been knocked into one; and that made this a big place. He had heard about building work being done here, but hadn't even suspected the extent of it. He did know that Hemmingway had questioned the builders closely, to find out if anything had been bricked up, or whether there were secret safes or cellars where stolen goods could be stored.

Hemmingway asked: "Dawson upstairs?"

"Yes, sir."

"Mrs. Lee?"

"Yes, sir."

"Thanks," said Hemmingway. He led the way up, and the two big men were a tight fit on the narrow staircase. It was a new one, Gideon saw, and beautifully made. The panelled wallpaper was the most expensive money could buy. The carpet was thick and their footsteps made no sound.

Suddenly the baby started to cry again, and a moment later a woman appeared, carrying and crooning to a bundle in her arms. But this was not Lee's widow: this was a woman of middle-age, wearing too much make-up, and tight-fitting clothes. The baby only murmured, now. The woman had been a beauty once, and tried not to forget it, but the only real beauty left to her was in bright, deep blue eyes.

"Which one of you is Mr. Gideon?" she demanded, still rocking the baby in her arms, unexpectedly maternal in her manner.

"I am, madam."

"I'm Mr. Lee's mother-in-law," the woman announced. "If you've a Christian thought in your head, Mr. Gideon, you won't worry my daughter with questions now, she's had a terrible shock."

"We won't keep her a moment longer than we have to," Gideon promised.

"You don't have to worry her at all!" The woman's fine eyes flashed and her voice barked, but all the time she rocked the babe, gently. "Frisky was right, from what I can see, you police are all the same."

"We just have to do our job," Gideon said. "We have to find who killed—"

"You don't have to find anybody," Lee's mother-in-law declared. "It was Ratsy, he was so crazy he didn't know what he was doing."

"Positive it was Roden?" Gideon demanded.

"Don't be so bloody smart," she retorted. "I didn't see him, if I had I'd have stopped the rat. But the way he was carrying on about Frisky last night is enough for me, foaming at the mouth, he was, and Frisky did everything for him, absolutely everything."

"Exactly how did Roden 'carry on'?" asked Gideon.

"He behaved like a mad thing, that's how he carried on, said he'd kill Frisky if it was the last thing he did. Frisky just thought he was blowing his top. But I can't stand here gassing any longer. You just give my Ada a chance to get over this terrible shock, that's all."

She turned back into the room she had come from.

Hemmingway whispered: "Frisky must have had some good qualities, to let a ma-in-law like that live with them."

Gideon made no comment.

The landing here had been extended, too, and Gideon saw the landings of the other two houses; quite a job of reconstruction. He saw a small book-lined room through an open doorway, and the glimpse told him that it wouldn't shame anyone. Hemmingway led the way along a passage leading to the front of the house, and said: "Frisky's been sleeping alone since the baby arrived, his wife had the kid in her room. That's how it was she didn't find out what had happened until late. Got up, fed the kid, made some tea and took it into Frisky, and then she saw—"

Hemmingway had a love of the dramatic, often without realising it. He finished outside an open door which was guarded by a uniformed policeman. Two men were inside when Gideon stepped in to see exactly what Mrs. Lee had seen.

It almost turned his stomach.

Lee had been lying on his back. The first slash of the knife had probably killed him, but there had been many more slashes. Blood, drying and congealing to a dark brown, now, was everywhere; it splashed the wall, it even splashed the cream-coloured carpet. Wherever there were splashes there were chalk marks on the wall; obviously the photographers and the fingerprint men had been busy here, and the job was nearly done. Two men at the window gave Gideon the impression that they'd been at it for a long time.

"Enough to unhinge her," Hemmingway remarked.

"Yes," agreed Gideon, and didn't look away from the man on the bed, although he had to clench his teeth. "Anything spring to your mind when you first saw this?"

Hemmingway frowned.

"Plenty."

"Hate."

"Eh?"

"Whoever killed him hated him, or wanted it to look as if he did," said Gideon.

"Ah," muttered Hemmingway. "He was asleep, obviously didn't move or do anything to try to fend the chap off, so the first blow killed him. Cartoid artery. And then slash and slash again. Yes. Depends on the strength of the blows a lot, I suppose." He rubbed his chin slowly, very thoughtfully, then looked across at the man at the window. "You got anything?"

"Someone came through this window all right," the man

said. "Scratches all over the paint, one or two fingerprint blurs, too, we might be able to get something."

Hemmingway nodded. Gideon stepped across to the window, examined the scratches, and remembered the footprint on the window at Chilton Court, of the woman who had climbed to her death—backwards. This window overlooked the backs of small houses, and the blank wall of a warehouse which was only two storeys high. There were window-sills and big pipes below, and it would not be difficult to climb up, for any man who was nimble and not nervous. Gideon wondered whether it was possible to check if these marks had been made by someone coming in or climbing out, but he did not ask the question then. All these things had to be looked at first, but he was anxious to talk to Mrs. Lee.

"Any signs of breaking and entering downstairs or the other rooms?"

"No."

"Be a help when we know whose prints they are," said Gideon, looking at several smears of grey powder. It was very hot, and he was sweating as he turned away. In the distance he could hear the buzz of sound in the street markets.

"Going to talk to Mrs. Lee before Gabby Lyon comes?" Hemmingway asked. "Lee's ma-in-law will have sent for him by now."

"Yes," said Gideon. "Your chaps are turning the place inside out, aren't they?"

"If there's anything to find here, we'll find it," Hemmingway asserted. "I've always wanted to see Frisky your way, remember."

He tapped sharply at a door across the landing, and a woman called thinly: "Come in." Then the baby cried in another room, and the grandmother with the flashing eyes began to croon again.

Hemmingway thrust open the door.

Frisky Lee's widow sat, alone, in a winged armchair in a corner of a large room – so large that obviously two rooms had been knocked into one. It was beautiful; and in spite of her pallor and the look in her eyes, Mrs. Lee had real beauty, too. Her hands were resting lightly on the arms of the chair, and she looked almost as if she was made of marble. She wore a pale rose-pink robe, high at the neck, superbly shaped at breasts and waist, and falling about her legs to the floor in great folds.

The window was open. This room was at the front of the house, so the sounds of the market came in more clearly, raucous though distant, and there was no quiet.

The room was panelled in satin. The single bed had a canopy at its head, and satin panels, too. By the side, empty, was one of the most beautiful cribs Gideon had ever seen, all pale blue muslin and lace for Frisky Lee's son. On each panel of the wall was a reproduction of a Gainsborough or something very like it. The furniture was exquisite reproduction of the Louis XV period. The room might belong to the wife of a millionaire, and here sat Frisky Lee's widow, in the heart of the East End of London, with its drabness and its squalor, its poverty and distress.

Mrs. Lee stared at Gideon.

Hemmingway said: "This is Commander Gideon, from Scotland Yard."

"I'm very sorry about this, Mrs. Lee," Gideon said, almost perfunctorily. "Do you know who did it?"

She didn't look away from him.

"I can't help you," she said. "I don't know who did it. I don't know anything." She spoke quite well, with only a faint undertone of Cockney; but either she was numb with shock, or she was going to play dumb.

"You must be able to help us, Mrs. Lee. Do you—"

"I can't help you, I don't know anything," she insisted. "I can't help you at all."

That was when Gideon sensed the truth; and Hemmingway did, too. The woman was afraid to talk. The dead hand of her husband was heavy upon her, as it had lain upon so many others. Could he hope to break her down?

Gideon asked abruptly: "Did your husband have a woman

friend?"

"No!"

"Are you sure?"

"He loved me, he was faithful to me."

"Quite sure?"

"Of course I'm sure."

"Have you a lover?" Gideon demanded, harsh and accusing.

She cried: "No, no! What an awful thing to say!"

"Have you a lover?"

"What are you talking about? What—"

"I want to know who killed him," Gideon said roughly. "I don't want his murderer to get away. Who hated your husband, Mrs. Lee?"

"No—no one hated him."

"Who hated him?"

"No one!"

"Did you hate him?"

"No, I didn't, I loved him!" She jumped up from her chair and stood in front of it, hands clenched, eyes blazing, in exactly the attitude he had hoped she would adopt. Her restraint was going, her self-control had almost gone, soon she would begin to cry; and crying, talk. Gideon was a policeman, first and last, his job to find the killer, and if she could help him he must make her. "Don't stand there and accuse me of killing him," she cried. "I loved him!"

"Someone hated him."

"I didn't, I loved him." She took a step forward, and shook her fist at Gideon. Anger had brought colour to her cheeks and put life into her eyes. She was trembling, too; she was almost magnificent. "No one hated him except you bloody coppers, even when he was trying to run straight you wouldn't let him."

"Mrs. Lee, someone killed your husband. You saw what they did. Remember?" She dropped back a pace, and raised a hand to her face, as if to shut out a vision of horror. Gideon almost regretted his cruelty, but went on without a pause: "I want to know who hated him like that. All you have to do is tell me."

She said in a low-pitched voice, as if words hurt her now: "No one hated him, and I loved him."

"Why try to protect a murderer, Mrs. Lee?"

She didn't answer.

"That is what you're doing," Gideon accused. "You are protecting the man who killed Frisky. If you loved him, you owe it to his memory—"

There was someone coining up the stairs; voices; a man speaking quietly, saying: "I know my rights." Someone called up, loudly: "Mr. Hemmingway, Mr. Lyon insists on coming up."

Gideon was disappointed and annoyed but not angry; this was a continuing battle between the police and the powerful forces ranged on Frisky Lee's side. There was time for one more effort.

"Come on," Gideon rasped. "Who was it?"

"I don't know!"

"Was it Ratsy?"

He made her look at him, and saw the absolute look of astonishment in her eyes, as if she was bewildered by the question. But he wasn't fooled. He felt sure that she knew who had killed her husband; he was almost sure that he knew why she dared not talk.

Then her mother's shrill voice sounded outside.

"Well, you've taken your time, I must say."

Gideon caught a glimpse of Ada Lee's mother, without the baby now, with exaggeratedly pointed breasts and a remarkably small waist; she would have passed for Ada's sister anywhere. And the sharpness of her tongue was not reserved for the police: it was used on Gabriel Lyon, too.

Lyon came in, a smallish, middle-aged man with a lot of iron-grey hair. He was immaculate, and had an air of confidence and assurance, a charming manner as well as a pleasant expression. He ignored Gideon and Hemmingway as he crossed the room, both hands outstretched. Mrs. Lee moved towards him, the colour receding from her cheeks.

The young grandmother watched with those very bright eyes.

"My dear Ada, I'm so very, very sorry," Lyon said. He held her hands gently, and she stood with him until he guided her back to the chair. "I shall do everything I can to help," he promised her, "and I know the police will, too."

He looked round at Gideon.

"Won't you?" he asked.

"Bah!" ejaculated Ada's mother, and walked away, as if nauseated; but her going proved her trust in Lyon.

"We'll find the killer quicker if Mrs. Lee tells us everything she knows," Gideon retorted.

Lyon spread his hands. "You can be quite sure that she will give you all the information she can, but she must have your sympathy now, Mr. Gideon. Her doctor will soon be here, and I'm sure he will order her complete rest."

"Mr. Lyon, don't get in our way over this investigation," Gideon said. "We're going to dig deep into Lee's past, and we're going to uncover a lot of queer business. Don't get in our way."

"I shall be anxious to help you in every way I can," Lyon said, still smoothly. "Now, if you will be good enough to allow me to have a few minutes alone with Mrs. Lee, I would appreciate it."

A man, hurrying up the stairs, broke across his words.

Gideon and Hemmingway were already on the move towards the doorway, when the man appeared; a sweaty, red-faced plainclothes man from the Division.

"We've found—" he began to blurt out.

"Hold it!" Gideon snapped, and actually hustled Hemmingway out, and closed the door; at least Lyon and the woman need not know what had been discovered. "Keep your voice low," he ordered. "What have you found?"

"Dozens of wallets and purses, cheap rings, fountain-pens, hundreds of things that have been knocked off," the man reported, and he could not keep the excitement out of his face or his voice. "They were in Ratsy's room, under some loose floorboards. Looks like a pickpocket's hoard. Who'd have thought we'd find stuff like that at Frisky Lee's?"

"C'm on, George," Hemmingway breathed. "Let's have a dekko."

Three detectives were in the small room, which was spotlessly clean and well lighted. More hiding places had been found, some containing stolen jewels, others empty cases and boxes; but the one big hoard was enough to go on with. Fingerprint men were already testing some of the wallets, but Gideon, handling one, felt pretty sure of one thing they would find.

There were children's prints on most of these.

There were children's prints on nearly all of the shiny surfaces. The loot of the child criminals had been brought here.

"We'll keep quiet about this," Gideon ordered. "The less Lyon knows the better."

"What a hell of a shame Frisky's dead," Hemmingway said, almost ludicrous in his longing to have a live Lee to charge with being in possession of these stolen goods. "Know what I think, George? We've only just touched the surface. They were in Ratsy's room as a plant, of course – we'll never fasten this on to Lee."

10

GIDEON GOES HOME

Nothing else incriminating was found, but men were still searching when Gideon and Hemmingway left.

"Never been able to make my mind up about Gabby Lyon," said Hemmingway. "Sometimes I think he's the biggest crook this side of Aldgate Pump, and sometimes I think he's on the side of the angels." They were entering his office upstairs at NE Divisional Headquarters.

"Know what you mean," said Gideon. "Open a window, Hemmy, it's like an oven in here."

Hemmingway thrust up a window, which opened on to the yard of the police station, where only one car was parked. Then the Divisional man moved to his desk, where there were several reports and photographs. His lips puckered into a whistle. Gideon sat on the corner of the desk and tried to be patient.

"Ratsy's prints on the handle of the knife, Ratsy's prints on the window frame of Lee's window, and on a newly painted drainpipe outside." He shot an almost excited glance at Gideon. "Here's some more. Ratsy was seen leaving the house about five o'clock this morning, by the front door, and seen to go back towards the back of the house about half-past six. The doc gives the approximate time of death as seven o'clock – not much later, anyhow. Looks as if Ratsy was thrown out of the house after a row, went to Tod Cowan's and begged for a couch, crept out again when Tod had gone back to bed, then took his revenge on Frisky. If he lost his head, he'd show his hatred all right."

"No definite indication of the cause of Ratsy's death yet, is there?" Gideon asked.

"Give us a chance."

"Just hoping," said Gideon mildly. "If he wanted to kill, why didn't he do it before he left Lee's house?"

"What's the matter with you, want it in words of three letters?" demanded Hemmingway. "He left, turned up at Tod's place and established what he would call an alibi. Then he crept back. Not much difficulty about that, and Ratsy was the best man at climbing a wall in this Division."

Gideon nodded, but didn't speak.

"You yourself asked who hated Frisky," Hemmingway said, "and God knows Ratsy had reason to. He was always getting the raw edge of Lee's tongue, often the thick end of his boot, too. Everyone knew he was bound to turn sooner or later, and we've got the mother-in-law's evidence about his mood,"

"Oh, yes," Gideon agreed. "Want to know something?"

"Try me."

"I don't want Ratsy to be the killer," Gideon said. "That would be too easy. I want the killer to be someone who's worked with Frisky Lee for a long time, who can still hold the lid on this mess, until we get him."

"See what you mean," conceded Hemmingway. "But evidence is evidence, George. Wonder if we've picked up anyone trying to sell hot stuff yet?"

"What we want is a second-in-command," Gideon went on. "When we get him, we can find out who's training these kids, and what else is going on."

A telephone rang as he finished, and Hemmingway picked it up.

"Superintendent speaking." He listened for a moment, then his face brightened up, and he grinned across at Gideon. "Go on—who else? . . . I see, okay. Yes, keep off Fraser all the morning, and the others. Ta." He rang off and his grin was the grin of a happy man. "That was the C.I. who's watching Mick Fraser. We've got the house surrounded. Picked up three boys on the way to him with hot stuff in their pockets, hoping to unload and get a bit of cash before everyone knows about Frisky Lee. Gee-Gee, this is going to be one of the big mornings!"

"Somebody has to have some luck," said Gideon. "Want me any more?"

"No, but let's go downstairs and have a pint," suggested Hemmingway. "I can do with a wet, wouldn't mind a sandwich, either. Might hear the cause of Ratsy's death before we've finished, too." He led the way downstairs, looking bright and cheerful because the things that he had always wanted to happen, were happening: crooks who had done their jobs and had been sitting on the loot for days, weeks and even months were going to try to unload this morning. At least three were booked for a long stretch, and with luck there would be dozens more. Whichever way one considered it, much of the credit would come Hemmingway's way; it looked as if he would retire in a blaze of glory, and with his Division cleaned up as well as it would ever be.

They had beer and some hefty ham sandwiches.

The cause of Ratsy's death was still not known when Gideon left the Divisional office, but within five minutes of entering his own, at the Yard, there was a call from a satisfied, almost a smug Hemmingway.

"Ratsy died from natural causes, that's established," he said. "He's been under the doctor for cardiac troubles for years. Any sudden or unusual exertion brought on an attack, and this one was fatal. Two more witnesses turned up who saw him coming away from the back of Lee's house, too. It's all cut and dried, George. And we picked up two more of the boys with their pockets full of loot, this time at Robo's place. What's the betting we won't get that dozen before the day's out?"

"Keep it up," said Gideon. "Thanks, Hemmy." He rang off, and sat back in his big chair for a long time, his face greasy with sweat, the tie hanging down and the ends of his collar loose. His face was set and hard. He picked up the pipe which he hadn't lit all morning, groped for matches and struck a light. He remembered the look in Mrs. Lee's eyes when he had mentioned Ratsy as a possible killer, and felt more than ever sure that she thought she knew who the murderer was, and certainly did not suspect Ratsy.

He picked up a telephone, and said: "See if you can get me Mr. Gabriel Lyon, at his Whitechapel High Street address, or else at 3, Medd Alley, Aldgate – the name there is Lee. Let me know what happens." He rang off, and drew at the pipe; and it was sweet. He dabbed his forehead again, looked out at the grey skies and wondered if the storm, obviously on the way, would cool the city.

Then he pulled a note-pad towards him, and jotted down several things, including the fact that he had seen that cowed boy from Hyde Park in the Lane that morning.

The indications were that Lee had become so bold that he had used his own house as a storage place for stolen goods. There was a possibility that the loot had been planted, but it was not very great. Obviously he, Gideon, ought to be feeling very pleased with himself. If Lee's death sent all those thieves rushing to sell their stuff, then Lee's part was absolutely certain: this was complete vindication of all his theories.

Yes, he ought to be feeling cock-a-hoop.

A telephone bell rang.

"Mr. Gabriel Lyon, sir."

"Where'd you find him?"

"At the Medd Alley address, sir."

"Thanks. Put him on." So Lyon had been with Mrs. Lee for nearly three hours already. "Hallo, Mr. Lyon."

"Good afternoon, Commander," said Lyon, in his pleasant voice. "How can I help yo?"

"You can tell Mrs. Lee that she needn't worry about anything happening to her baby, we'll see to that. She'll be quite safe if she'll tell us who killed her husband."

Lyon was silent for a moment, obviously not expecting such bluntness.

"I'm serious," Gideon went on.

"I'm sure you are," said Lyon, as if perplexed. "I had no idea that you or anyone else seriously thought that Mrs. Lee knew who had killed poor Lee. As you know, she's quite distraught, and I've had a doctor to see her. He's given her a sedative, and insists that she must be kept quiet and without visitors for the rest of the day. The moment I can talk to her, I will find out whether she is frightened."

Was he a smooth-tongued hypocrite?

"All right, if that's the best you can do." Gideon did not sound enthusiastic.

"Before you ring off," said Lyon, "I wonder if I may ask you this: have you any grounds for believing that the baby has been threatened?"

"I think Mrs. Lee is frightened, and mothers frighten easily over their children. Mr. Lyon, have you noticed the recent crop of child pickpockets?"

"Yes, and deplored it greatly."

"Know where they're being trained?"

"If I had any idea, I would inform you," Lyon assured him. "Good afternoon, Mr. Gideon."

"Good-bye," said Gideon.

It was half-past four. Tea would be ready at home, the younger children would be on their way back from Sunday School, Prudence and Penelope would be out with their boyfriends, Kate would be relaxing. He had done plenty for a Sunday, and every possible angle was being checked. He had to remember that his was really an office job, he could not be out on the prowl, much though he sometimes longed to be. And he had to remember that Lee, the fences, and the pickpocket ring, were only part of the overall picture. He must not let it obsess him. He called the Yard exchange, and said: "Telephone Mrs.

Gideon, and tell her I'll be home, hungry, in about half an hour, will you?"

"Yes, sir."

"Thanks," said Gideon.

At Brighton, Marion Carne had a wonderful day, and Robert now seemed as enthusiastic as she about the business they were to start very soon.

At his home, Dick Sparrow worried his problem, feeling sure that Dennis had driven his wife to her death, but not seeing the slightest chance of bringing it home to him.

At Hyde Park, on this, his Sunday off, Police Constable William Smith was hanging about, hoping to see the boy and the vicious woman; so far, none of the plainclothes men had been able to help him.

In three different parts of England the police investigated reports that Sheila Crow and her father had been seen, and each report proved false. In London, Mrs. Crow, still with her sister, went about as if in a dream-world.

Not very far from Petticoat Lane, Peter Wray was in the cupboard, crying, his back raw from strokes with a knotted rope. He had failed that morning; worse, he had nearly been caught dipping his hand into a woman's handbag.

Throughout the East End police there was jubilation, for already fourteen thieves who had been sitting on their loot, knowing that the cooler it was before they sold it the more valuable it would be, had been caught approaching the homes of known fences. They were all broke; none of them could have lasted much longer without some cash, and they had made a desperate attempt to get some before the police traps went into operation.

Hemmingway drew up a comprehensive report, which virtually put the onus of the murder of Frisky Lee on to Ratsy Roden, although the inquests were yet to be held and most of the formalities were still to come.

At the three-in-one luxury house in Medd Alley, the police searched intensively, but found nothing more to help. Ada Lee's mother remained aggressively in charge of the baby and her daughter and two servants went about in silence, the room where Lee had been killed was sealed off, and the room opposite was sealed almost as tightly by one of Lyon's girl clerks, who was at the door ostensibly to go in if Mrs. Lee wanted anything.

On the bed, Ada Lee lay in a kind of coma, not really unconscious, not really conscious.

At Eastbourne, several local police constables and a gravedigger cursed Superintendent Warr of the Yard, because he chose that evening for the exhumation of a man who had been dead for six months. It was done successfully, and attracted little attention; it wouldn't be long before the Press took the exhumations up in a big way, Warr believed, not knowing that the Press had a huge story coming with the murder of Frisky Lee.

What Warr didn't know, and no one yet knew, was that the housekeeper of four dead men, Martha Smallwood, had slipped quietly to church that evening, and walked away afterwards, in the darkness, when a Detective there to watch her was distracted by a busty girl.

Martha Smallwood had a comfortable place to go.

She had an elderly friend, a gentleman in the late seventies, who lived alone in a bungalow near Bognor. He was nearly blind, and could not read or see the newspapers. He had few friends, and did not even know about the death of the four other old men who had been so like himself.

He was fond of Martha, who was known to him as Martha Smith.

She had promised to come and keep house for him.

11

REMANDS

The atmosphere at Scotland Yard could change almost overnight, sometimes in the course of an hour or two. No place was more rife with rumour, few people outside listened with such close attention to it. Few people were more sensitive, either, in the sense that the police were aware of both criticism and hostile comment. All except the very new men in the Force were hardened to it, all pretended that it did not matter what the Press said, the public thought, and Parliament blathered about; but in fact it mattered a great deal. Undoubtedly the Press stimulated the C.I.D., even if at times the newspaper angles caused annoyance and occasionally anger.

Things had been flat for most of the Yard during the past few weeks. Sunday's events transformed the situation.

The little back room door on the Embankment was thronged with newspapermen from noon on Sunday onwards. Any officer believed to be engaged on the Lee case, and the subsequent arrests, was stopped and questioned by a reporter. The Monday morning headlines brought a glint to every policeman's eye, and probably gave Hemmingway his greatest day while in the Force – his greatest day in thirty-five years.

POLICE SWOOP ON EAST END

ran the headlines.

WAR AGAINST CRIME FLARES UP
20 ARRESTS AND MORE TO FOLLOW
THOUSANDS OF POUNDS WORTH OF STOLEN PROPERTY
RECOVERED.

The stories differed but the hard core was the same. The murder of Frisky Lee had given the police a chance to stage a great clean-up in the East End, and the police had been ready. Under the direction of Superintendent Hemmingway, with Commander Gideon in the background, hundreds of houses had been visited, thousands of people questioned, many more arrests could be confidently expected.

Every man at the Yard read this, and the change in the atmosphere was remarkable. Men walked more briskly, Squad drivers drove with more pep, men on the beat paid closer attention to any slight detail which might be suspicious. The mood spread quickly from the Yard to the Divisions. The Old Man was summoned to the Commissioner's office, where a pundit from the Home Office had come in person to congratulate the Criminal Investigation Department.

Gideon would have been at this jam session but for the fact that he was at the East End Magistrate's Court. Sixteen men were accused of having stolen goods in their possession, and the police asked for a remand in each case. The magistrate granted eight days, in custody. No solicitor spoke for any of the men, only two asked for bail, and that more from impudence than hopefulness. Gideon looked round the court and saw the worried faces of the women in the public gallery, the nods and smiles from the men in the dock to these women. He sensed the gloom and the tragedy and the impending misery, yet in spite of the problems unsolved, he felt the stimulus of what had happened, and shook hands warmly with Hemmingway at the request of the Press photographers who swarmed round. There were even two newsreel cameras.

And Gideon could not find it in himself to question Hemmingway's judgment openly. The inquests on Lee and Ratsy would be held tomorrow, anyway. He drove back to the Yard, and among the messages waiting for him was: "Mr. Gabriel Lyon called, and will call again at twelve noon."

"Didn't say what he wanted, did he?" Gideon asked Lemaitre.

"Said he wanted to talk to you personally," Lemaitre told him. "Let him wait; Warr's back, and if you ask me, Smooth-faced Sydney's got a load of worry."

"Oh, lor'," said Gideon. It was then twelve noon exactly, and the telephone rang. He lifted it, but spoke to Lemaitre. "What about?"

"He wants to keep it for your ears alone," said Lemaitre.

"Gideon," said Gideon, into the telephone. "Oh, yes, put Mr. Lyon through." He saw the door begin to open, and watched the big, plump man as he came in, slowly, soft-footed, smiling. Warr was always worried when he gave that set smile.

"Good morning, Mr. Lyon." Gideon decided to be affable.

"Ah, Commander," said Lyon. "I'm glad I've caught you. I have to go out of town for a day or two, and I was anxious to speak to you first. I talked about that matter to Mrs. Lee, and she assured me that she has no reason at all to fear that harm might come to her child. I do assure you that you have been misinformed. Both she and her mother have, however, told me – and the police, I'm glad to say – about the quarrel which her husband had with Arthur Roden during the early hours. Apparently Roden was caught stealing some loose change, and Mr. Lee dismissed him summarily. Roden appears to have had a brainstorm. A great tragedy, but—" Lyon left the rest in the air.

Gideon could take it or leave it.

"Mr. Lyon," he said.

"Yes, Commander?"

"Mr. Lee had a reputation which wasn't exactly enviable, and we now know for certain that he engaged in criminal activities. The circumstances of this crime make it not only possible but imperative that we conduct a thorough search and inventory at the house in Medd Alley. We shall be in possession for about a week. I don't know whether you will advise Mrs. Lee to leave for that period, or not. I want to make absolutely sure that there is no evidence that others had motives for killing Mr. Lee, and that Roden, if he actually killed Mr. Lee, wasn't paid to do so by someone else."

"I quite see your point of view," said Lyon easily. "I shall advise Mrs. Lee and her mother to leave the house entirely at your disposal. Good-bye."

Gideon hung up, pushed the telephone away, and said to Lemaitre: "Take anything that comes in, Lem." He handed cigarettes kept for visitors across the desk to Warr. He had to switch his attention completely, emptying his mind of the Lee affair, and because he did not particularly like Warr as a person, he made a special effort to be both fair and friendly. And he realised one thing which not everyone admitted: Warr was exceptionally conscientious, probably much more so than many better and more likeable officers.

"Something gone wrong?" Gideon asked.

"George, I'm worried about two things, and part of it is my own fault." The confessional. "Martha Smallwood went to church last night, and the local chap watching her didn't keep his mind on the job, and didn't see her come out. Two or three elderly women were dressed more or less alike, and he followed the wrong woman. Martha S. must have gone through the vestry, or a side entrance."

"Oh, hell," thought Gideon, as he said: "She shouldn't be so hard to pick up."

"That's what I thought. I set the local chaps looking everywhere for her, felt sure that she'd only gone to a neighbour. I couldn't think she'd have the nerve to disappear, so I didn't report at once. She's still missing."

"Want a general call, eh?" said Gideon, and looked across at Lemaitre, who was listening eagerly. "Fix that, Lem, you've got the Smallwood woman's description."

"Okay."

"Think she might throw herself in the river or off a pier?" Gideon asked Warr.

"I shouldn't think she's the suicide type, although you can never tell," said Warr. He hadn't really got everything off his chest yet, although he was a little easier in his manner. "I've dug up several more things I kept to myself, thought I might as well make a comprehensive report when I made one."

Here came the really bad news.

"What else have you found?" asked Gideon.

"She's made a habit of taking on several jobs at the same time," said Warr. "She'd be officially housekeeper to one old man, and go and do a bit of reading during her time off for someone else. That way she's got a circle of old men acquaintances, all of them thinking she's wonderful. She's benefited from at least four old people's wills, and there may be more, because she's used at least three names. The worst"— Warr gulped—"the worst of it is that the furthest back I've been able to trace is seven years."

"Seven years!" echoed Gideon.

Lemaitre was trying to give instructions over the telephone and listen in at the same time. In the middle of a request for the call for Martha Smallwood, he ejaculated: "Seven!"

"No telling when she really did start, either," added Warr gloomily.

The easiest thing in the world would be to tell him what to do, tell him to hurry, make him feel that he had really lost the initiative. Gideon's mind was racing over this, but he sat there as stolidly as ever, fingering the rough bowl of his pipe after that one outburst.

"What do you want to do?" he asked at last.

"I'd like Martha S.'s picture in every newspaper as well as the general call, and an invitation to the public to tell us about any elderly men who've known her," Warr said. "That's going to be a hell of a job, we'll need two or three men on it all the time, just sifting the correspondence, but—"

"Needs doing," agreed Gideon. "Lem, who've we got?"

Lemaitre had finished his telephone calls.

"Charley Rowe," he said. "Him and Freddy, they'll be just right for this job."

"Can you spare them?" Warr asked Gideon, and had never shown greater eagerness.

"I'll tell 'em to drop whatever they're doing, and work with you on this," said Gideon promptly. "The quicker we can pick Martha S. up the better." He soft-pedalled almost to a point of pomposity. "Anything else, Syd?"

"It depends," said Warr, and he smoothed his white forehead with his damp, pale hand. "No doubt that the three bodies we've exhumed tell a tale, George. Some damn bad post-mortem work in one, and in two the doctors gave a death certificate in good faith. I will say this, she only seems to finish off those who are on the point of going, anyhow." He stood up. "Thanks a lot, George."

Now the newspapers had more banner headlines, and the stories of the wholesale remands in East London were squeezed off most of the front pages.

YARD SEEKS MISSING HOUSEKEEPER

Scotland Yard Superintendent Sydney Warr and Chief Inspectors Rowe and Wildsmith are working on one of the most remarkable investigations of the century. The bodies of four men, each of whom was old and frail, have been exhumed, following investigations into the death of Charles Henderson, eighty-year-old retired bank manager. Henderson's housekeeper, Mrs. Martha Smallwood, is being sought by the police, as she may be able to help them in their inquiries. Mrs. Smallwood was last seen at Evensong on Sunday, when . . .

"Here we go," said Lemaitre, reading the newspapers next morning. "No sign of Martha yet, though. Wonder where the hell she's gone?" Gideon grunted.

"How anyone can have the bloody nerve to kill people off like this I don't know," said Lemaitre, "and it's no use telling me I'm jumping to conclusions, she bumped these old boys off."

"Looks like it," agreed Gideon. "After the first one or two, it must have seemed so easy she probably didn't think twice. It'd become habit. Warr thinks she might be with an old man, now."

"She'd never do it again!"

"Is she sane or is she mad?" asked Gideon. "All I know is that Warr's going to have to organise a countrywide visit to every man over seventy who lives alone, and that's going to be some job."

"And last week you took time off," marvelled Lemaitre. "How many over-seventies do you think there are? Half a million? Well, that's only about five or six calls per copper, on the national average."

"I know one thing we can do," said Gideon. "We can run this with a search for Sheila Crow and her father."

"Could do," agreed Lemaitre.

Then his and Gideon's main telephones rang, and they lifted them at the same moment.

Gideon found himself with a split-second hope that this was more news from Lee's place, and a lead to the children's training school; it was a routine question, that was all. Routine, routine, routine.

At Bognor, not far from the sea, in one of a colony of little bungalows which looked very like one another, an elderly man, frail and nearly blind, sat basking in the window, with the sun shining gently on him. Close to his chair was his white stick. Close to his hand was a radio, playing light music. It was nearly one o'clock, and before long the news would be on. He heard his new housekeeper bustling about in the kitchen, and when she came in, he smiled round at her.

"Everything all right, Martha?"

"Course it is, why shouldn't it be?" Martha said, and began to lay the table. He could not see her expression when the B.B.C. announcer began the news, he did know that she stayed in the room longer than he expected, while the headlines were being read; all he liked to hear were the headlines. He preferred her to read the news to him from the newspapers, later in the day.

"Scotland Yard officers . . ." began the announcer.

Flick! And his voice went dead.

"I can't bear hearing about these murderers," Martha said, "there are so many of them these days it's enough to give you the creeps. Now turn your chair round, Percy, and wheel it up to the table. I'll have lunch in a brace of shakes."

She went bustling off.

The radio stayed dead.

For Gideon and the Yard it was a week of exceptional activity. The East End job, preparing cases against so many known thieves, getting witnesses, taking statements, making raid after raid on people named by the men who were charged, would have been enough in itself, but was nothing compared with the daily task of sorting out the negative reports about the housekeeper and the Crow father and daughter. Friday was the record day; one thousand and twenty-seven different reports were received, saying that a woman answering Martha Smallwood's description had worked for old men who had since died. To anyone unused to the avalanche of reports which sometimes came in from the public, it would have been almost frightening. At the Yard, the two C.I.s and a staff of two elderly Detective Officers and a girl typist sorted out the reports, the dates, the places, the names of the men, the ages, details of when and how they had died, all relevant information. On that day, Friday, two hundred and fifteen photographs of different women were received, and each of them tallied approximately with the description of official "photograph of Martha Smallwood". By that day, also, over ten thousand calls on private houses had been made by policemen throughout the country in search for the woman, and no trace of her had yet been found. No incidental news came of the missing Sheila Crow, either.

"If you ask me," said Lemaitre, "Martha's changed her appearance a lot, that's easier for old women than anyone else; no one's surprised if an old girl wears a wig." He rubbed the back of his neck. "She must go and eat *some*where."

Martha Smallwood was still missing at the week-end.

Sheila Crow and her father were missing, too.

Marion Carne was happier than she had ever been, for she had seen the showrooms and offices they were to rent for the new business.

Sparrow pondered most days over Reginald Dennis, but Eve Dennis was buried, and there seemed no justification for making any more inquiries.

Peter Wray had a bad week, spending in all twenty-three hours in the cupboard. In the seven days since the Petticoat Lane morning, he had eaten nine "meals", three of them of dry bread and water.

The search of Frisky Lee's house led nowhere; dozens of known pickpockets were questioned and none admitted knowing a thing. One complained bitterly about the kids working on his beat. There were no adult prints on the stolen goods, but prints of four children already caught were identified. Few women had visited Lee's house, nothing suggested that it had been used to train the children.

None of the thieves had ever dealt direct with Frisky Lee; none admitted having known his wife. They simply "knew" Lee was the fence. All had taken their goods to Petticoat Lane, in the middle of the Sunday morning rush, and unloaded there.

Hemmingway asked the same questions a hundred times.

"Who took the stuff and who handed you the money?"

Invariably the answer was the same: a woman. Some said she was in her early thirties, some said she was in her fifties. That wasn't a case of confused descriptions: different women, acting as Lee's agents, had bought the stolen jewels.

And different women trained their children . . .

"That's a new line," Gideon said, eagerly for him. "Lem, tell every Divisional Super to have these mothers questioned, try to find a connection with Lee or Lee's wife."

Ada Lee stayed with her mother during the police "occupation", and had no visitors. She still seemed to be grieving, but her baby flourished.

The coroner's inquest verdicts were what the Press and the police expected: that Mark Matthew Lee had been murdered by some person or persons unknown, but there was insufficient evidence to say by whom, and that Ratsy Roden had died from natural causes.

There were the cases of cruelty, the suicides, the wife murders, the wife beaters, the Teddy Boy outrages, the cruelty to animal cases, the small felonies like shop-lifting and bag-snatching and pocket-picking – everything was exactly the same; it was a rubber stamp of a week.

"No one would ever think it of you, George," Kate Gideon said on the Sunday evening, "but you take it too much to heart. You can't work miracles."

"Don't want to work miracles," Gideon said, pulling at his pipe. The television play was a dead loss. "I'd just like to find that Crow child, I want the Smallwood woman, and I want to find out the truth about the Lee business, and whether kids are still being trained for the pickpocket jobs. As a matter of fact I'm more worried about the Smallwood woman than anything else at the moment. Do you know how many men we *know* she's worked for, now?"

"How many?"

"Twelve, over an eight-year period," Gideon said. "Now tell

me I ought to read a nice book."

Kate said practically: "Well, sitting there brooding won't help, and it's possible that they'll have found her by the morning."

"Martha," said the old man.

"What is it, dear?"

"Do you feel all right?"

"Of course I feel all right."

"I don't think that fish we had for supper was as fresh as it could have been."

"Nonsense," Martha said, "it was as fresh as a daisy."

Quick Joe Mann's daughter had three women working in her back room that day, and Quick Joe became an even better tutor. He always finished with the same piece of advice: "The younger your kids are the better they become, and the younger they are the more sentimental people feel towards them. In my experience, if you start training' them at six or seven, by the time they're eight or so, they never make a mistake, and never get caught. Now, there's one other thing. You aren't to take any stuff to Petticoat Lane until I tell you, hold on as long as you can, and if you're really hard up, I'll buy some goods off you."

12

THE THIRD MONDAY

Depression seldom lasted with Gideon for long. At ten o'clock, Pru the violinist and Penelope came in together, flushed and excited over a concert they'd been to with their boyfriends, attractive and eager, both of them favouring Kate more than Gideon. It was one of the evenings when he realised that his elder daughters were young, marriageable women, and Penelope, who looked more like him, would be soon. Matthew, all set for his first year at a University, and determined, he insisted, to join the Metropolitan Police when he'd finished with all this nonsense of education, came in just afterwards, after seeing a film. He had a gift for mimicry, especially of Americans, and soon began to act the fool. Gideon found himself laughing almost against his will; and then found the arms of contentment closing about him.

He needn't keep his job at home with him all the time.

He woke early on that third Monday in the month, with a sense of keen anticipation, for fourteen of the East End cases were coming up, and the case against each crook was ready; there was no doubt that each of the accused would be committed for trial, the evidence made sure that none could hope for acquittal. There was a kind of exhilaration in getting so many charges together, and if no more good came out of the death of

Frisky Lee, this was good cause for satisfaction.

The magistrate almost used a rubber stamp.

The crowd outside the court was the largest Gideon could remember, and among the people present was Gabriel Lyon. Gideon was getting into his car, with a battery of cameras trained on him, when a sleek young man came up, and said: "Excuse me, sir, Mr. Lyon says if you could spare him half an hour later in the day, he would be grateful."

"Where?"

"Would Mrs. Lee's house be convenient, sir?"

"Three to three-thirty," Gideon said.

"That will be all right, sir, any time."

Gideon drove straight back to the Yard, made a note of the appointment, and checked the messages on his desk. Only one managed to switch his thoughts from Lyon and the Lee business:

P.C. William Smith, 27532, telephoned and will telephone again at 12.45.

It was then 12.30. Smith and the peaky, pale-faced and frightened lad who was almost certainly being taught to pick pockets. Nothing else that really interested Gideon came in, until a telephone rang, and he lifted the receiver almost without thinking, and said: "Gideon."

"George." This was the rather nasal voice of a Divisional man in FI Division, on the south-eastern fringe; there was only one voice like it in London.

"Hallo, Fred?"

"Got some bad news for you."

"You being transferred to the Yard?"

"I'm serious," the Superintendent said, "you being you, this is bad. We've found Sheila Crow and her father."

Number 41, Crystal Street, London, N.E., was like thousands of other houses in the vicinity. They had been built between the wars, and the builder had thrown them all up, much as one would rabbit hutches, and many had been the complaints of jerry-building. After thirty to forty years, and after some of the severest bombing of the Second World War, all except those houses which had received a direct hit were still standing firm. A few walls were slightly cracked, and some plaster was cracking, but the gardens were mostly gay.

The one thing which made Number 41 stand out was its garden, which was ill-kept. The lawn hadn't been cut for over a month, bushes were overgrown, early spring flowers were leggy. The windows needed cleaning, too, and no one quite understood why there wasn't a FOR SALE or TO LET notice showing in the front garden. The owner did not live in the district, and that perhaps explained it. All kinds of rumours were spread, including the "fact" that the owner was going to live in it himself, or that his "daughter" was going to get married and come and live there. The nearer neighbours, who felt that the unkempt garden was a reflection on their own efforts, were annoyed by all this, but small children found that the garden was a useful place for cowboys and Indians, cops and robbers, and hiding from their parents.

A woman from four doors away could not find her six-year-old son, and she called and then went to look for him and, as a consequence, was the first adult to pass the back door of Number 41 for two weeks. The curtains were drawn. She also noticed that there was a kind of packing at the windows which looked a little odd, and there was one thing which really vexed her. One of the windows was broken, obviously with a stone or a cricket ball. She saw her son and two other children pretending to hide behind bushes at the end of the garden, and called crossly:

"Keith, come here!" Keith started at once. "Did you do this?" She watched him hang his head, and blessed the fact that he would not lie. Her heart warmed so much that it was difficult to keep the stern note in her voice. "Keith, why *do* you throw stones near houses? I'm always telling you, and what your father will say I just don't know."

Keith came on more boldly, and the other children appeared, apparently quite carefree.

She scolded them.

It was while she did so that she smelt the gas.

She had noticed a peculiar smell before, but hadn't really identified it; now suddenly she realised that it was gas. All at once, the packing at the window made sense. Cautiously she went nearer to the window, and the smell of gas became much stronger. She pushed the curtain aside gingerly, and a moment later saw the man and the girl child lying on the floor.

Then she knew why the smell had been peculiar.

"Come on, all of you," she said to the children, and tried not to give way until she was in the street, safely away from horror. "Keith, the front door is open, go straight in and get washed in time for"—she almost choked—"supper. Tommy, you and Kathy must go home at once, your mother will be so worried. I'm just going to have a word with Mrs. McKeon."

Mrs. McKeon's house had a telephone.

The police were at Number 41 within ten minutes, quickly followed by the ambulance and a police surgeon.

". . . yes, it's Crow, all right," said the FI Divisional Superintendent. "He and the kid have been there ever since they disappeared, our medic, says that they've been dead at least fourteen days. Crow owned the house, apparently, but told no one. He went there and put the child to sleep and then pushed her head in the gas oven, and laid down beside her. They'd had a meal, some milk and some chocolate, I don't expect the kid knew anything about it. Hell of a thing, gas ought to be turned off in all empty houses, can't understand why it wasn't in this one."

Gideon said: "All right, thanks."

"Job out at Hammersmith," Lemaitre said, a few minutes

afterwards. "Treasurer of a thrift club tried to drown himself, one of our chaps pulled him out of the river. He'd pinched fifty quid. Who'd kill hisself for fifty quid?"

"Hmm."

"George."

"Yes?"

"Think I could take a day off tomorrow?"

Gideon looked up. "Why not, Lem? Take a couple, if you want 'em."

"One's enough." Lemaitre almost smirked, and Gideon half wondered why, but he couldn't get Mrs. Crow's face out of his mind's eye. Then Dick Sparrow telephoned, taking him from one form of failure to another; a worried and reluctant Sparrow, who said: "All right for five minutes, George?"

"Fire away."

"I've gone over the evidence in the Dennis case with a fine-toothed comb, half a dozen times," Sparrow said. "I still think Dennis knows something, but I don't see how we can make a case. There's just that footprint or two, the scraped shoes, and the fact that Dennis inherits – not that that's surprising. I think we'll have to drop it, George. But will you have a look at the papers, if I send 'em over, and let me know if you think there's anything we might follow up?"

"Yes, Dick, right away."

"Thanks. Anything up?"

"Found that Crow girl and her father, he seems to have killed her and committed suicide," Gideon said.

There was a pause.

"What goes on in a man's mind to do it, that's what I can't understand," Sparrow said. "Why, my kids—" He broke off. "Okay, George. 'Bye."

"'Bye."

Gideon rang off. One thing that Sparrow had said made him ponder: it wasn't surprising that Dennis inherited his young wife's fortune, because she had died intestate. She hadn't willed it to him. The clever ones didn't plan to benefit through wills, it often looked too obvious. The clever ones tried to get their hands on the money first, and the accident or mysterious death happened afterwards. God knew how many times a thing like the Dennis affair passed unsuspected.

"There it is," said Marion Carne, her face so happy and her eyes so bright. "*The Carne Agency – Everything for Motor Cars.* And there's our joint account, darling, and the estate agent says he's sure we can have those showrooms and offices if we want them. I know the rent is a bit high, but you've always said yourself that it's no use spoiling the ship for a ha'porth of tar. I like them very much."

"Yes, they're the right premises," Robert Carne agreed. "All right, darling, we'll go and see them about it in the morning."

"Lovely!" Marion said eagerly. "Now I must go and get my hair done, it won't do if I start looking a wreck, will it?"

Carne laughed, kissed her, and went to the door with her.

He returned to the small room in the hotel where they were staying, drew up an armchair, lit a cigarette, and frowned at his reflection in the dressing-table mirror. He began to think aloud, in a very low-pitched voice.

"I can take that twelve thousand and clear off with it, and the worst she could do is to kick up a fuss – it's mine now, as well as hers. Or I can hold on for a bit, and fix her, and have the lot. Thirty thousand quid isn't to be sneezed at. The trouble is, how to do it and get away with it? There must *be* a way;"

Gideon said: "Gideon here," as he lifted the telephone, and remembered almost at once that P.C. William Smith had summoned up enough courage to telephone him. Smith obviously believed that he knew something of importance, or he wouldn't have dared to call the Commander. Gideon knew exactly what attitude to adopt: not over-friendly, or it might encourage the man too much and make him big-headed; not stand-offish, or it might make Smith freeze up.

"That you, Smith?"

"Yes—yes, sir," Smith said, and undoubtedly he was very much on edge. "Hope it's all right to call you, sir, but I didn't quite know what else to do."

"What's on your mind?" Gideon asked.

"It's that boy, sir – you remember."

"Yes, of course. Found him?"

"Well, I haven't found him, sir, but one of the plainclothes chaps – a friend of mine, as a matter of fact – found out his name. Wray. He was following the mother, and someone used the name, sir. That was in Petticoat Lane, yesterday morning."

So the boy had been there two Sundays running.

"Is that all?" Gideon tried not to sound as if it was hardly worth the fuss.

"Well, no, sir, as a matter of fact—" Smith hesitated at the crux of his story, probably because he was afraid that it wasn't much of a climax. "Apparently the woman who talked to the boy's mother is a well-known pickpocket, sir, and—"

Ah.

"Yes?" Gideon uttered the single word in such a way that it gave Smith all the encouragement he could want, and he spoke much more freely.

"She's known to train children in the game, sir, she's been inside twice for that. Of course it may mean nothing, but I'm not sure what I should do next. It's not on my beat, but over at Aldgate, and the woman hasn't been in the park for a couple of weeks."

"I see," said Gideon, "and you've been checking in your own time and don't want to poach. That it?"

"Exactly, sir!" The answer came more brightly.

"Put in a report to your own plainclothes branch," said Gideon. "Give them full details, tell them that I first asked you to keep your eyes open. I'll fix it with Mr. Hemmingway of NE, and he won't mind whether you've been poaching or not. Right, Smith."

"Thank you very much, sir!"

"S'all right," said Gideon, and rang off. He made a note to

talk to both Smith's Divisional Chief, at AB, and Hemmingway, to get things moving. With luck, the Wray woman would be known. There was a spark of hope that she might lead them to the main training source.

The telephone bell rang.

"Gideon."

"Mr. Warr is on the line, sir, from Brighton."

"Put him through . . ." There was a brief pause. "Hallo, Syd, had any luck yet?"

"If you mean, have we found Martha, no," said Warr, but he did not sound as glum as that seemed to warrant. "What we have found is her bank, and the name she goes by there. She paid in three hundred and seventy-five pounds under that name the day after Henderson's death, and the bank still has some of the notes, they were put aside in a reserve stock. They're quite positively part of Henderson's money. And what's more—"

"Yes?" Warr obviously wanted prompting.

"She transferred her account to Brighton from Hastings, two years ago," said Warr, "so I'm asking the Hastings people to step up the pace a bit."

"Fine," said Gideon. "Keep after 'em."

But Hastings was a long way from Bognor.

Old Percy Whitehead, in his Bognor cottage, had recovered from his indisposition after eating the fish, and had almost forgotten the incident. But he was a little puzzled. It was true that he wasn't overfond of the news, but he had little to do but take notice and think, and could hardly fail to notice that Martha always switched off the radio just before the news, or before the headlines were finished.

He was not consciously suspicious; not consciously uneasy. He just wondered why.

He wondered about another thing, too.

A lot of people were fooled into believing that because he was so nearly blind, he did not notice things. He probably noticed much more than people with good sight, because anything in an unfamiliar place was a puzzle and sometimes an inconvenience; it could even be a danger. Now he knew that most of the things in his bedroom had been moved; even the corners of the carpet had been turned up. Of course, Martha might have been cleaning the bungalow without telling him, but usually she was full of talk, explaining what she was planning to do and what she had just finished, and how badly the bungalow had been kept.

She was nice and cheerful and friendly, but she was a human being, and Percy Whitehead knew a great deal about the frailty of human nature where money was concerned. He wondered if she was looking for anything, and whether at any time he could have been fool enough even to hint to her that he had nearly a thousand pounds in cash hidden in the bungalow.

13

HONEST MAN?

Gideon, being far too big a man to pass unnoticed anywhere, made no attempt to hide the fact that he was going to Medd Alley that afternoon. As it happened, the Press and the local police were surfeited with the morning's East End Court news, the official watch had now been withdrawn from Medd Alley, and no one took much notice when his car turned into the lane, and he got out and stepped quickly to the door of the middle of the three which had been recently painted. This was a collector's museum of a house, with its tastefulness and its smell of death and the three-month-old child and the beautiful woman who lived here.

Ada Lee's mother opened the door.

If she made-up less, she would be really attractive; it was easy to see from where her daughter had inherited her beauty, and her shining eyes were quite remarkable.

"If I was Gabby Lyon, the only place I'd talk to you would be in court," she said waspishly.

"Mother, please don't make a fuss." Ada Lee was just behind her, protesting, but without vigour. Gideon ignored her mother and studied the young widow. He wished he could spot the real truth about her lack of vitality, her dullness. Was it grief? Or was it fear?

Her mother had ten times the vitality.

Gideon went to the middle room, which Lee had used as a study.

Gabriel Lyon was sitting in a high-backed chair at Lee's desk, and at sight of Gideon, he stood up slowly, rounded the desk, and held out his hand. "The man in possession," thought Gideon, and reminded himself that Lyon was Mrs. Lee's legal adviser, and that the estate was valued at some two hundred thousand pounds. So far, the police could not touch it; so far, Frisky Lee was still, in law, an honest man.

"It's very good of you to come, Commander, won't you sit down?"

"Thanks. Can't imagine you asking me for the sake of gossip," said Gideon, and shook his head when cigarettes were proffered. "No, thanks." The case was a gold one; Lyon's finger-nails were painted with natural colour varnish; and his tailor must be one of the best in London.

"As a matter of fact, Commander, there are two things I want to talk to you about," said Lyon, "and I felt it would be wise if we had a little quiet talk, quite unofficial. In this part of the world, and having the clients I do, it would be unfortunate if anyone suspected that I was leaning too heavily on your side, wouldn't it?"

Crafty?

"I see what you mean."

"We understand each other," murmured Lyon. "The first thing is about Mrs. Lee. You will recall that I scoffed at the possibility that she was frightened, or that the child was in any danger. In fact I was annoyed because I thought that you were being unnecessarily thorough."

"Have to be thorough," said Gideon flatly.

"Commander," said Lyon, glancing at the closed door and lowering his voice, as if to make sure that he wasn't overheard, "the simple truth is that although Mrs. Lee says that she has nothing to fear, she shows an abnormal anxiety for the baby. I am fully aware that it might be a consequence of shock and loss

– any woman who has lost a devoted husband would quite naturally be very possessive indeed. But I'm not satisfied that's the only cause. I asked Mrs. Lee's mother if she had noticed it, and she had. Mrs. Lee will not allow the child out of her sight, and even refuses to take it out for a walk, saying that it might catch cold. She also hesitates to leave the child alone with its grandmother, who naturally feels that this is ridiculous. They have been very sharp with each other about it." Lyon looked steadily into Gideon's eyes, and went on more slowly: "Had you any reason for suggesting that she might be under some threat?"

Gideon thought: *"Is he honest?"*

Perhaps Lyon really wanted to know, so as to warn anyone who might be concerned; there was no way of telling. Taken at his face value, he was co-operating perfectly; had this been a man in a different part of London and with a different list of clients, Gideon would have taken him at his face value more readily.

"I wasn't satisfied that Roden would kill without being pushed into it," Gideon said, "that's all."

"I see. Well, it is a fact that Mrs. Lee is extremely possessive and apparently frightened for the child. I've discussed it with her doctor."

"What does he say?"

"He suggests a complete rest," Lyon said. "Somewhere at the seaside or in the country, where she can relax."

"It's the kind of thing that's been suggested before," Gideon said dryly, "and she can afford it."

"Yes," agreed Lyon, and drew back a little, as if he knew that he couldn't draw Gideon out any further. "But I doubt if she'll go. Well, that is the main thing I wanted to say. I'm sorry you haven't more specific reasons for suspicion, because I want to make quite sure that Mrs. Lee is given every opportunity to recover. The other matter is very different, however. Commander, I will tell you what very few people know: I lost my only son, at the age of six."

Gideon didn't speak, but remembered the son he and Kate had lost.

"I find it an obligation to defend many people who have committed serious crimes, and when I weigh up all the circumstances, of their environment and their inherited weaknesses, I don't find that difficult," Lyon went on. "You won't want platitudes, but you would be astonished if you knew how often I say to myself: 'there but for the grace of God go I'. But I cannot and I will not tolerate the abuse of children if I can prevent it. There is a limit to what one man can do, of course, a limit even to the things I hear. But I have known for some time that there are more child pickpockets and shoplifters in London today than there have been for many years, and you raised this matter the other day."

"Yes?" Gideon tried to hide his quickening interest.

"Were you aware that there is a kind of central organisation – the children taught mostly by women, often their mothers – who in turn attend a kind of training college, and pass on what they learn to the children?"

Lyon's narrowing eyes seemed to reflect the light so that he looked challenging and almost angry. He sat quite still, the back of the chair an inch higher than his grey head, and he didn't look away.

"We know it exists," Gideon said, and leaned forward heavily. "We know that the stolen goods are mostly brought to Petticoat Lane, and we also know that a hoard was found in Lee's house."

Lyon seemed to wince.

"Is that official?"

"It's a fact. I'll tell you some more facts, Mr. Lyon. For a long time thieves of all kinds have been to Petticoat Lane with their stolen goods, and women – probably these perfect mothers – are taking them and paying for them. I believe they were working for Frisky Lee, but I can't prove it, yet. I can prove that Lee terrorised a lot of thieves, and he was hated by many of them. We don't yet know which one killed Lee."

It was impossible to judge Lyon's reaction, because he showed no reaction at all, and his eyes were narrowed but unwinking. Whatever side of the fence he was on, this could do no harm and might do a lot of good. If Lyon was honest, this would shake him. If he was working for the other side, it would warn him how close the police were to the truth.

Lyon raised both hands, in a gesture almost of supplication.

"Commander, my duty is to the living. I can tell you that Mr. Lee paid out a number of pensions, as he called them, in cash. You can guess whether they were pensions or payments for services rendered. On the list was a certain Quick Joe Mann, at one time the most skilful pickpocket in London."

"Quick Joe," echoed Gideon, and felt a moment of intense elation. "Anyone else?"

"I think Joe is quite enough," Lyon said.

Quick Joe smiled perkily at one of the two women in the back sewing-room at his daughter's house, and asked her to walk towards him, holding her handbag over her arm. She left her sewing-machine, and obeyed. She was handsome and brassy-haired, with a fine figure, and obviously she was enjoying herself. As she passed him, Joe hardly seemed to move; there was no sound. But when she glanced down she saw her handbag gaping open, and her purse in Quick Joe's hand.

"It's a question of the quickness of the hand deceiving the eye," explained Joe. "I began this trick at the age of five, and by the time I was seven no one in London could touch me at it. Remember that selection of the victim is of first importance, and in the early days a pupil must be told who to approach. You should simply indicate the victim, and leave the rest to the child. The first essential in the child is absolute obedience, of course, the strictest discipline must be imposed." Joe beamed. "No use sparing the rod, is there? Now supposing you see if you can do this on Clara's handbag?"

The other woman stepped forward but before she acted, Joe's daughter called up from the narrow hall: "Joe, look out of the window."

Something in her tone made Quick Joe step to the window. He saw two plainclothes men climbing the wall to the tiny back garden, and others moving in from adjoining gardens. He turned in dismay, suddenly very pale.

"Start working on those hems," he ordered, "never mind if you make a mess of them, get the sewing-machines going. If the police ask questions, don't say a word except that you're working for Liz. Get it? That's all you've got to say." He stepped swiftly to the door, opened it, and saw tall, lean Woodrow, of QR Division, at the head of the stairs; shock upon shock. He tried to smile. "Why, Mr. Woodrow, surely you know you've no right to force your way into a house like this?"

"Like to see my search warrant?" Woodrow waved a slip of paper in front of Quick Joe's face. "We're on to you, Joe, you might as well talk and make it easy for yourself."

"My dear Mr. Woodrow!" Joe sounded plaintively outraged. "I am a guest in my own daughter's house, and—"

"Joe, we've been watching you," Woodrow said, "and we've discovered that five of the women who've worked for your daughter have children who've been picked up for bag-snatching or dipping. Let's have the names and addresses of the rest of them, and let's know who buys the stuff from you."

"You're talking out of the back of your neck," Joe asserted, but he was too nervous to be impressive.

Five minutes later, the police found the contents of a dozen handbags, some purses and several wallets, all emptied, on top of a cupboard.

"All right, all right, I can see it's no use arguing," Joe submitted uneasily, "but don't blame *me*, Woodrow, it was Frisky Lee who made me do it. I'd been on the level for a coupla years, I had, then he put on the pressure about an old job I'd done years ago. Said he'd squeal if I didn't oblige him. So I had to teach these women, didn't I? But"—he sounded shrill—"how did I know they were going to tell their *children* what to do? If I'd *dreamed* they were going to corrupt the minds of innocent young children, I wouldn't have raised a hand to help them, Frisky or no Frisky."

False virtue shone in the cunning old face.

"Joe," said Woodrow, "we're going to pick up all of these women, and they'll tell us the truth. And the only thing that might help you is the truth, too. How did you get the stuff to Frisky?"

"I never touched any stuff while he was alive, it was only after he died I helped the women, just to oblige," Quick Joe declared. "If it hadn't been for that, I wouldn't have been copped; if I knew who killed Lee I'd tell you like a shot."

"Who killed him, Joe?"

"I tell you I dunno? If I did I'd tell you." Joe's voice was almost a squeak.

"How did the women get their stuff to Lee?"

"They took it to the Lane, he had several women working for him there. Used one stall one week-end, another the next, and the stall-holders were too scared not to allow it. These women took the stuff and flogged it, that's all I know."

"The stall-holders had a cut for their trouble, the woman go-between had a cut, and the rest went to Lee. Is that it?" Woodrow asked.

"Lee always got sixty per cent, never less. Tight-fisted old swine, that's what Lee was."

"Who was his share paid to, Joe?"

"How do I know," shrieked Old Joe. "How do I know?"

"Joe," said Woodrow softly, "Lee had an agent in the Lane. This agent collected Lee's share of the cash. Who was the agent?"

"It was Ratsy Roden," Old Joe gasped, and the sweat was heavy on his forehead and his upper lip. "As I stand here, it was Ratsy. He was a runner for Lee, that's what he was. We all knew it was Lee who took the rake-off, but we couldn't prove it, could we?"

Gideon listened . . .

"The truth is, we still can't hang anything on to Lee, even now he's dead," he said at last. "We haven't finished the job yet by a long way. Got a list of these mothers?"

"Eleven in all, so far," Lemaitre answered. "He says he doesn't know where the others live."

"Let's have the list, and I'll see they're all called on," Gideon promised. "Anyone named Wray among them?"

"What name was that?"

"Wray, with a W."

"No," answered Woodrow, "the only W on the list is a White. Anything special about a woman called Wray?"

"Could be," said Gideon.

He instructed all the men who questioned the women to ask about a Mrs. Wray. None brought him news. All the women had young children, each had stolen goods on the premises, each blamed the children, claiming huskily or stridently that they were out of control. But Quick Joe and his daughter were damning witnesses, now.

"We'll put every one of these women on a charge," Gideon said to Lemaitre, "but we'd better check with the Public Prosecutor's office to find out how we can hurt 'em most. If we can prise 'em loose from their kids, it'll be the main thing."

"Yup," said Lemaitre, and went on: "Think Ratsy did collect the money and take it to Lee?"

"He could have," Gideon conceded, "but if Ratsy took it straight to Lee, I'll eat my hat. Lee wouldn't take the risk. Ratsy may have been the collector, but he'd take it to a third party. If we keep digging, we'll find out who.

I'm going over to see Hemmingway again," he declared; "before this is over he'll hate the sight of me."

"Trouble with you is you're never satisfied," Lemaitre remarked, but he spoke to a closed door.

Gideon sat in his car outside the Yard for a few minutes, thinking of Lemaitre's words. "Never satisfied." What was there to be satisfied about? The child, Wray, was still missing.

Little Sheila Crow, murdered, and they'd taken two weeks to find out. Anguish for a mother. A girl probably pushed off a window-sill to her death, and all the police could do was shake their heads and be sorry that they couldn't tackle the killer. Dennis had killed his wife all right. A mild, little helpless-seeming creature like Martha Smallwood could go to church and vanish. Ratsy could die and be blamed for murder he almost certainly hadn't committed

All this burned through his mind as he sat there; and it was a long time before he felt calmer. Then he started the engine and moved off to see Hemmingway, going past Medd Alley.

He glanced along it from a corner.

Frisky Lee's widow was watching him from a first-floor window.

A frightened Ada Lee?

He'd thought so. Lyon couldn't have made it plainer that he thought so, too, but Hemmingway, the coroner, everyone at the Yard and the Division and in the newspaper world believed that Ratsy Roden had killed Lee. He, Gideon, didn't. And now there was evidence, so insidiously offered by Lyon, that behind his veneer of good behaviour, Lee had been subsidising a training school for child thieves.

He flicked on the radio.

"Tell Chief Inspector Lemaitre that I'm going to see Mr. Hemmingway, and then I'm going over to Mr. Woodrow at QR. Check if I'm wanted for anything, will you?"

"Yes, Mr. Gideon."

He waited. He wasn't wanted. He drove off, and a policeman nearby saw the speed with which he started, and said: "Something's got into Gee-Gee today, that's a sure thing."

14

PATIENCE

The difficulty was to be patient. Perhaps Hemmingway was the wrong man to see in his present mood, although it was essential to talk to him. Hemmingway was like a dog with two tails. He had never had such a good press, never made such a clean sweep, and seemed to think the millennium had come. He had only a couple of months of service left, Gideon reminded himself, and police officers didn't come any better.

"Damn' remarkable thing happened when I got back here after the Big Court, George," Hemmingway announced. "You'd never guess."

"What?"

"People outside raised a cheer. How about that?"

"Good work," Gideon said, and tried to look as if he thought it wonderful, while wondering how he could persuade Hemmingway to do what he wanted. "You've got how long left in the Force, Hemmy?"

"Seven weeks and four days."

In spite of himself, Gideon chuckled.

"Then the happy land of deckchairs and gardens," he said. "I wish everyone had the same chance of going out in a blaze of glory as you have."

"I've got enough, thanks!"

"There's a bit left," Gideon said.

"Well, leave it to the new chap. Any idea who's coming here?"

"No," said Gideon. In fact he had a shrewd idea, but there were some things which had to be left to the Old Man and the secretary; everyone had some preserves it was dangerous to poach on. "You know what a stubborn ass I can be."

"Hallo, hallo, hallo!" exclaimed Hemmingway, "I thought you'd got something on your mind. What is it?"

"I want to know who put Ratsy up to killing Lee," Gideon said.

"Oh, dammit, George—"

"Have a go," urged Gideon, "and let me tell you why. Mrs. Lee's so frightened that she jumps at the sight of her own shadow, she won't allow the baby out for a walk, she's even quarrelling with her own mother about it. That could add up to mental illness, or it could add up to the fact that she's been threatened. I want to know."

Hemmingway raised his hands and shrugged.

"You want to know," he said, "and you'll know. All right, George, I'll have another try. Anything special you want me to do?"

"Just worry it," said Gideon, and then went on almost casually: "There's one thing I'm going to do; put a chap from one of the other Divisions on to watching both Mrs. Lee and her mother, so that they aren't covered by anyone who'll be recognised as a policeman. And find out the best way to make the mother talk."

"She's a bitch," Hemmingway said, "and nothing will make her do what she doesn't want to. If you ask me, she's as scared as Ada is, and they'll both keep quiet."

Uneasily, Gideon thought: "He's so happy that he just wants to keep clear of trouble and please everyone." But there was nothing more he could reasonably do, and he still hadn't any clear-cut idea on how to get at Lee's killer; or at the people who were frightening Mrs. Lee. It was rather like the Dennis job; he was sure of the truth but couldn't pin it down. Queer thing, how

Ratsy had died when he had, so very conveniently. Queer thing—

My God!

Conveniently.

"Now what's on your mind?" said Hemmingway, seeing his expression change, and speaking almost resignedly. "When you start getting ideas I know there's going to be no peace for anyone."

"Hemmy, how closely have you checked Tod Cowan lately?"

"Well, since you ask, I haven't checked him, always assumed he's on the level," answered Hemmingway. "I've never had a thing against him in all my time here, except that he's been in the Lane and when you mix with that mob, you get your hands dirty."

"That's it," Gideon said. "We've known him so long we take him for granted. We might have slipped up."

Hemmingway wasn't impressed.

"Well, I agree Tod's in as good a position as anyone in London to sell stolen clothes, but we've checked his stock dozens of times and never found anything that shouldn't be there. His wife makes sure he keeps on the straight and narrow, she's twice his size, and squashes him." Gideon had a mental picture of the fat, bulgy woman with her dyed hair in metal curlers, by the side of little Tod Cowan. "I admit that all we did on this job was to get Tod's statement, and check it with a couple of others from people who saw Ratsy come in and then leave again," Hemmingway went on.

"Oh, Ratsy went into Tod's shop, and left in a hurry," conceded Gideon, "but what drove him out? See it this way, Hemmy: he had a flaming row with Frisky Lee, ostensibly for stealing petty cash. I can believe he'd steal, I can even believe Lee would throw him out on his ear, assuming that Ratsy didn't pay over the money he collected direct to Frisky. We know Ratsy took refuge at Tod's and we all tell ourselves what a reliable chap Tod is. But what forced Ratsy out again? Only overwhelming pressure would have driven him out of the shop

and back into Lee's house. It was in the early hours of the
morning. Ratsy was tired. He crawled into that chair-bed. You
and I know that nothing would ever make Ratsy work if he
could avoid it, and after a session like that he'd be in a state of
prostration. Yet something made him get up and go out again
– and the only people inside the shop, or living over it, were old
Cowan and his wife. Right?"

"Right," agreed Hemmingway, and raised his hands and
looked towards the ceihng with mock piety. "Thank Gawd
there's only one George Gideon. You know what, George?"

"What?"

"I was only joking with Tod the other day, 'Tod,' I said,
'you're making too much profit out of those second-hand glad-
rags of yours, that's a nice mink coat you've got your wife.' And
he grinned at me and said: 'Got it at trade price, Mr.
Hemmingway, and Minnie's waited thirty years for it.' Tell you
what, George. I'll find out the value of that mink coat, and find
out where she got it from, too."

"Let me know quick," urged Gideon.

He left soon afterwards, knowing now that Hemmingway
was launched on the job he would move really fast, for he
would want to vindicate his own prowess. Gideon drove
towards the Tower and Tower Bridge, heading for the river by
a short cut which would take him past the Mint, and then along
Tower Hill. No one was on the hill, it was late for the lunch-
hour speakers, but the car-parks were full, and it looked as if
the Tower was having its daily stint of visitors. He thought he
saw one of the ravens on top of a building, the sun glistening
on its wings, and then drove along Eastcheap, eventually to
Billingsgate where the smell of fish was very strong, round by
the Monument and at last to London Bridge. He did this simply
because it was London and he didn't often get out this way.
London soothed him, the centuries-old buildings, the narrow
streets, the square round the Monument with the tale of the
Great Fire, helping to woo him into the proper frame of mind
for seeing Woodrow, the Superintendent at QR. He drove

slowly over London Bridge, glancing right and left at the shipping, some of it masted, and then fell to the overpowering desire to stop the car and go and look over the parapet of the bridge into the Pool of London, the ships of all nations, the busy, bustling cranes, the tugs, the small boats, the low buildings. He had not been there for two minutes before a policeman came up, stepping out quite smartly.

"No parking on the bridge," the officer said, courteously enough. "Not planning to stay, sir, are you?"

"No. Sorry. I'll be off at once." Gideon saw recognition dawning in the other's eyes, and hoped the man wouldn't apologise for doing his job. He didn't, but touched the peak of his helmet. Gideon drove off, much calmer, cheered by the fact that that policeman had appeared so quickly, and had told him so courteously to get to hell off the bridge. The big span of the Tower Bridge began to open as Gideon drove away, and he wished he had timed his visit better.

He felt less troubled, now. Hemmingway had done him good, helped him to get a clearer perspective. There were dozens of inquiries going on, none which was likely to yield such results as Hemmy's job.

If only he could put his hands on the boy Wray.

Peter Wray's mother stood towering over the boy, holding his right wrist tightly, twisting enough to force his arm upwards so that if he so much as moved he would be in excruciating pain. His face was pasty white, his eyes looked huge and filled with dread.

"If a strange man ever speaks to you, what do you do?"

In a small, lost voice, the child said: "I go away, I don't answer him."

"Suppose he offers you sweets?"

"I say no thank you."

"What do you say if a copper asks you why you're not at school?"

"I say I've been ill."

"What do you say if a copper asks you where you've been?"

"I say I've been to the river looking at the boats."

"So you do," the woman said, and her lips tightened. Then, she raised her arm very slowly, and drew his up with it, forcing him to rise on tip-toe in an effort to ease the pressure on his arm and elbow. This drove everything but the look of pain from his lips, and put despair into his eyes, and he gasped because the pain became so great.

"What do you do if a stranger offers you sweets?"

"I—I—I say no thank you!"

"You little liar, you didn't say no thank you this afternoon, you took some," she said, and she flung his wrist free, then grabbed his shoulder so that he couldn't get away. "Don't lie to me. I know you've been eating sweets. How did you know it wasn't a copper? Go on, tell me that, how do you know?"

"I—I—I don't know."

"If I ever catch you taking a sweet from—" she began, but he could not stand there any longer, just turned and ran into the cupboard and shut himself in.

The woman went across, turned the key in the lock, and then went to the wall-larder, took out some ham, bread and butter, and sat down to eat. She washed the meal down with stout.

The door of Gideon's office opened, a Chief Inspector looked in cautiously, saw that Lemaitre was alone, and went in, but kept a hand on the door.

"What the devil's the matter with Gee-Gee this morning?" he asked.

"Didn't know anything was the matter with him," Lemaitre said, "unless the wet morning's making him skid a bit."

"Don't give me that," the other grumbled. "He's got everyone on the hop. What's on? Had a directive from the Old Man, or—"

"Charley," said Lemaitre pontifically, "all he's doing is keeping the Criminal Investigation Department on its toes, and from what I've seen that takes plenty of doing. You got any special grouse?"

"No, but they say the briefing this morning was like a court-martial."

Lemaitre grinned.

"He was in form, all right. I don't know what it is, but something's got under his skin or is pricking his conscience. Mind your step."

"You know what it is," the C.I. said sourly.

"Not this time I don't," asserted Lemaitre; and he meant exactly that. Then Gideon's firm and heavy footsteps sounded along the passage, and the C.I. went out, to make sure that he wasn't cornered. His "good morning, sir," would have won praise from a Lieutenant-Colonel.

Gideon came in.

"What did he want?"

"He wanted to know if you'd been rapped by the Old Man," said Lemaitre, grinning. He was more relaxed than he had been for a long time. "What's up, George?"

"I decided that everyone was getting slack around here," said Gideon, "and I don't know of any exceptions. Anything doing?"

"Hemmingway called, he's going to call back. Arkwright looked in. Don't know that I think you're wise to encourage the ranks to come and see you in person, George. There was that copper Smith, of—"

"Special circumstances," Gideon said. "Lem, we're going to bring this department up to scratch. I mean it. Quick Joe's been working at this for three years. The Lane's been used by Lee for over two years. Lee's wife's dead scared, and we don't know who's scaring her. We can't find that kid, Wray. Some jobs are difficult, but these shouldn't be. We've got slack. I've just seen the Assistant Commissioner, and laid on a special drive." Gideon sat down as a telephone rang, and eased his collar while he said: "Gideon." Lemaitre saw an intent look spring to his eyes, and he went on: "Hallo, Hemmy, what's the news? . . . *How* much? . . . No doubt about it? . . . Two thousand five hundred retail, seventeen-fifty in the trade . . . Think Tod's been making all that money legitimately?" He chuckled; the nearest to an expression of good humour that he had shown on this Wednesday morning of the third week in the month. "His wife didn't squash him, after all. We'll keep tabs on him, and do some checking on his recent movements and any new customers he's had," Gideon went on. "I'll send someone who isn't too well-known over there. We don't want to make it too obvious, yet . . . Okay, Hemmy, thanks."

He rang off.

"Tod Cowan's mink coat," he announced.

"In the Lane?"

"Yes."

"George Gideon, middle name Glue." Lemaitre looked away hastily. "But there are other jobs. Nothing in from Warr yet, amazing where Martha S. is. You've got to hand it to her for cunning." That obviously wasn't the right subject. "You heard about the chap who was run down in the Strand this morning after trying to hold up a till, didn't you? In hospital."

"I heard," said Gideon. "Lem, this office is going to be so busy for the next week or so that you won't know what's hit you. I want to go over every case we've had through our hands without getting results, and I want to make sure we didn't miss anything. I'm going to question every man in charge of every case, major or minor, and as many men who worked on the cases as seems necessary. I'm going to make sure that every man in the department digs deep into what he's been doing lately. I'm going to make sure that if anyone's slipped up or been slack, they themselves find out about it even if I don't. In other words, I want this department right on its toes, and I'm going to keep it there."

Lemaitre sat very still through all of this, which was spoken with a quiet emphasis that made it doubly impressive; the massive shape of Gideon, at his desk, added to the effect.

"Got it, Lem?"

"I've got it," sighed Lemaitre.

After the shock of Gideon's decision, none of the senior men showed any resentment. Gee-Gee might be a devil at times, but he was a fair devil. The extra work was keeping him far busier than any of the others. He was at the office for the rest of that week until nine and ten o'clock each night, and didn't once go out on his daily perambulation round London's Square Mile. He drove himself on with a single-minded intensity which compelled the admiration even of those who thought that it was a lot of fuss about nothing.

Hour after hour, with Superintendents, C.I.S, D.I.s and Sergeants, he went over the unsolved cases of the past few months; dozens of cases ranging from shop-lifting to shop breaking, embezzlement, violence, sexual offences, begging, burglary, fraud, every kind of crime in the calendar. He had always been remarkable for picking up the details of a job at second hand, and knowing as much as the men working on the job; and this faculty seemed to have improved. He analysed every investigation, sometimes alone, as often with Lemaitre's help; and when he had finished he called in the man in charge and suggested what new approach he should try.

The Yard seemed to gather itself up for a great concerted effort. At the end of the week, Gideon felt that everything that could reasonably be done to clear up the back-log of unsolved cases was done. Nothing new came in about the Lee case. Tod Cowan was under observation; so was his wife, and reports were coming in of regular customers who went to Tod's shop ostensibly to make payments for clothes bought on the never-never.

Each regular was being watched, too.

But that was mainly Hemmingway's job. Gideon had plenty more – like the countrywide investigation into the victims of the missing Martha Smallwood, and Arkwright's problem.

He had talked to Detective-Sergeant Arkwright, who had now discovered that a Robert Carne had got married on the first Monday of the month to a girl named Marion Lane, who had inherited a small fortune from her father, but the coincidence of the initials R. C. gave even Gideon, in his present raking mood, no real excuse to probe further into the early married days of Robert Carne.

On the Sunday, the third Sunday in the month, Gideon was at the office all day.

On that same Sunday, only three miles away from Scotland Yard, Marion Carne sat at a small table, with several documents in front of her, and signed each one; a clerk from the service flats was a witness.

She signed over half of her fortune to her husband as capital for the new business.

She now stood between a man who had already murdered one wife, and fifteen thousand pounds.

Gideon, at that very moment, was feeling a sense of grim satisfaction. The crop of arrests following the death of Frisky Lee was likely soon to be beaten, partly because of much heart-searching among his men and partly because of the suggestions he had made. But they hadn't found Martha Smallwood; they still didn't know the truth about Lee's murder. Ada Lee still behaved as if she was terrified; and the Wray woman and her child were still missing. He was a long way from content.

15

RESULTS

Peter Wray's mother was cold sober that Monday morning, for news travelled fast, and she knew that many of the women who had "studied" at Quick Joe's were under arrest. She hadn't given Joe her real name, and the women who bought the goods from her, at the market, didn't know it was Wray, either. She had to make sure that the police could not get hold of the boy, Peter, and question him. She wasn't quite sure of the best way to handle the brat.

There was the "home" in Stepney, a shocking place but where the principals kept within the law, and where the children, all believed to be backward, were kept clean and fed, presentable and terrified; no one there would talk to the police, and that might be the best place, but it would cost four pounds a week. She could pay for a week or two, but that might not be long enough, and Peter wasn't really worth keeping, now; for months it would be too dangerous to use him.She sat on the bed in the small back room, dirty-looking pillows behind her, hair tidy for once, lips set tightly, hands clenched on her lap.

If the police came for him, she could say he had gone into the country.

She could keep him in that cupboard . . .

She knew that if the police really became curious, they would search all cupboards, and she did not seriously think that she could shut the boy up there indefinitely, but she had to get rid of him somehow.

Of course, she herself could go away.

There was her sister, over in Wandsworth, where she could stay as long as she liked. She could get a job charring for a few weeks; it wasn't what she wanted but it would pay for her keep. Her sister wouldn't take the kid, though, that was certain.

There was only one safe thing to do: get rid of him altogether. In the old days they just knocked the unwanted kids on the head, tied a stone round their necks, and dumped them in the river.

She couldn't do that.

She could just walk out on him and disappear, leaving him locked up, and he—

If she did that, after teaching him such a lesson that he would never dare to say a word, it might be best. This wasn't much of a place, and she could always find some ways of picking up a living.

It would be two or three days before anyone found the kid in the locked cupboard, and by that time she would be a long way from London. Well, why not? Once she was safely away, she could telephone Ma Higgs, at the corner shop. Ma would come and let him out, and say nothing to anybody. Ma daren't talk, because too many people knew too much about how she made her money. Ma Higgs was an ever-ready buyer of the goods which Peter stole. She didn't pay high, but she paid cash, and if things were difficult she was always good for credit.

Peter's mother climbed off the bed.

She would give the kid something to eat, first, and then put some bread and some water in the cupboard. It wouldn't do if he died, because then the police would hunt until they found her; they wouldn't worry so much about her leaving the kid shut up.

She went to the cupboard, and opened it with a slow caution foreign to her. The boy lay on the floor, asleep. There was

144

something she didn't recognise at first, or even understand; a sweet, sugary kind of smell coming out of the darkness. She frowned, and peered closer: then she saw the bag of sweets close to the child's hand.

She raised her clenched fist viciously.

"If you've been taking sweets from strangers again, I'll—" she began to screech, and then broke off abruptly. It wouldn't do to wake him; sometimes he had crying fits. The little devil, though, defying her again, anyone would think he'd never learn.

She fetched half a loaf of stale bread and a big jug of water, put these in the cupboard, stared at the sweets again, and couldn't understand it; there was at least a quarter of a pound, and he'd certainly have eaten some; he must have had them in his pocket when she had put him in here last night after the warning from Quick Joe's envoy.

"Who'd give him sweets like that?" she wondered uneasily. "If someone's been befriending him, it might mean real trouble."

She didn't wake him, though; just shut and locked the door.

Then she put on her only dress, pushed a spare pair of shoes and a few other oddments in a bag, tucked the thirty-two pounds which was her entire fortune down the neck of her blouse, and looked round to make sure that she had forgotten nothing. Not a stick of the furniture was hers, and she had paid the rent up to the week before last; that wasn't too bad.

She went out, closing the landing door, which was never locked. She went downstairs quite boldly, not caring whether any of the other dozen people who lived here saw her or not; she would just get on a train and go off, and the Midlands was the best place. Birmingham was always good for casual work, and there were plenty of lorry drivers and labourers who liked a bit of cuddly company. She preferred Birmingham to the ports, too, she was always choosy.

She stepped into the drab street and went towards the main road, having to pass the corner shop on the way; and then she remembered that she hadn't any cigarettes, so she turned into the shop. Ma Higgs was there alone, totting up some figures, a little grey-haired woman who must have a fortune salted away. Apart from her fencing, she did a good trade, because she allowed "tick" to anyone who wanted it, up to a certain amount; and when the limit was reached, her customers had to buy from her in order to keep her sweet. Everything she sold was fresh, she was on good terms with the police, and the shop was clean. She herself had a scrubbed look and a smile which fooled a lot of people for much of the time.

"'Morning, Ma," the child's mother said heartily.

"Hallo, Janey, you're all poshed up this morning."

"Going to look for a job in the city," said Mrs. Wray, glibly, "the money's better up there."

"Well, you ought to know," said Mrs. Higgs. "What can I do for you?"

"Twenty *Diggers.*"

"Here you are, dear. But you'll soon have to divvy up some cash, or some goods, you know."

"Won't keep you much longer," promised Mrs. Wray, and then remembered that she would soon want Ma Higgs to do her a favour. "As a matter of fact, I'll pay ten bob off the slate now. Might as well get out of debt as quick as I can." She handed over a ten-shilling note. "And I'll soon have a few odds and ends to sell."

"I knew you was in the money," said Mrs. Higgs.

Peter's mother's expression hardened.

"I get along," she said in a brusque voice, "and I'll thank you to listen to no gossip."

"Keep your hair on," Ma Higgs retorted. "I can put two and two together, can't I? When your Peter comes in every day for half a pound of sweets, that speaks for itself, don't it?"

"He does *what*?" gasped Mrs. Wray.

"He comes in—" Ma Higgs broke off, her expression almost as comical as the other woman's, and then suddenly she burst into deep, genuine laughter. "Strike me, Janey, didn't you *know*? He's a chip off the old block, he is, lifting enough cash to buy his own sweets because his Ma won't give him any pocket money! You've got a promising young man there, my dear, but you're slipping, you shouldn't have let him get away with it."

Jane Wray was too startled to speak at first. Then gradually she realised what was expected of her, and forced herself to shake her fist as if in the child's face.

"I'll have the skin off his back, the little beast! I'll teach him—"

Ma Higgs was still highly amused; Jane Wray herself was shaken, and yet in a way relieved. She had been worried about the "strange men" who had given Peter sweets, and had taken it for granted that a policeman or one of the child welfare workers had been trying to win his confidence. It was a relief to know that he had bought his own, and preferred not to tell her that he had kept some of the stolen money. The little swine might have been feeding off the fat of the land, come to think of it he had been looking fatter lately.

She could break his neck!

It was half an hour later, when she was mingling with the crowd at Paddington Station, and waiting for a train to Birmingham, that her expression changed. She gave a little grin, almost of affection.

"Little devil, that's what he is. He'll be able to look after himself all right. He'll never be able to say I didn't teach him that. Live to thank me, he will. Wonder if I'll ever see him again?"

She went for her train, quite determined to telephone Ma Higgs, or, better still, drop her a postcard from somewhere and tell her to destroy it so that no one could find out where it had come from. Ma would do that all right.

The train was crowded; Jane Wray forgot Ma, Peter, the sweets and the shock in her anxiety to find a seat.

"How's it going, Lem?" Gideon asked Lemaitre, about the time

147

that the train steamed out of Paddington Station.

"Not so bad," said Lemaitre. "We're getting our hands on those women who acted as buyers, they all say that Ma Higgs put them on to the job. It won't be long before we pull Ma in."

Ma Higgs was totting up some takings figures, a few hours after the Wray woman had left, when a car drew up outside; she had a number of car-owning customers, and that didn't surprise her, but when she saw Superintendent Hemmingway himself approach, with one of his senior Inspectors, she knew that this wasn't a courtesy visit. She dabbed some powder on to her cheeks, thrust her shoulders back, and went forward to greet them with a bright smile.

"I am honoured, to be sure, Mr. Hemmingway, with you in the news so much lately, too. Am I too late to offer my congratulations?"

"Generous of you, Ma," said Hemmingway, with an old-fashioned smile. "Been along to Tod Cowan's much lately?"

"No more than usual."

"Friend of Mrs. Cowan?"

"Oh, yes, have been for years," Ma agreed airily.

"That's a pity," said Hemmingway. "We've picked up several of Mrs. Cowan's old friends, and they've all got themselves into the same kind of trouble, selling and receiving stolen goods. You wouldn't do such a thing, would you?"

"If you can find a single stolen item in my shop, may God strike me dead," exclaimed Mrs. Ma Higgs, and drew herself stiffly to her full height; she even managed to look angry. "And I won't listen to a friend of mine being insulted, either, you ought to know better."

"Mind if we have a look round?" Hemmingway asked.

"You've no right—"

"Ma," interrupted Hemmingway, "I can get a warrant in half an hour, and while I'm waiting, two men will keep you in sight. Mind if I have a look round?"

The glitter in her eyes told how much she both hated and

feared him.

". . . and they found masses of hot stuff in the shop, mostly under the counter," Lemaitre reported to Gideon, and roared with laughter. "Got a false bottom, her counter had! Customers used to come in, hand over a wallet or a bag, and if anyone else came in she'd drop it down a kind of letter box and value it when the shop was closed. She says she acted for a woman who had a stall in the Lane, not for Frisky. 'Mazing how they seem as anxious to protect Frisky now as they did when he was alive, isn't it?"

"Get anything else out of her?" Gideon demanded.

"Got this – practically every woman who trained with Quick Joe was a customer of Ma's. We're getting nearer, George. The sooner we tackle Tod in person the quicker we'll get results."

"We'll wait a bit. Does Ma Higgs know this Wray woman?"

"She says she doesn't, and she won't name anyone," Lemaitre said. "She's not the kind we'll break down either, there's no point in waiting."

"I want to see what happens when the news gets round that we've brought her in," Gideon said.

"Anything in from Warr yet?"

"If Warr doesn't pick Martha Smallwood up soon, he'll jump in front of a bus," Lemaitre said half-seriously. "It's really getting him down."

16

MISSING MONEY

Martha Smallwood had gone to the shops.

There was no way in which Percival Whitehead could tell the change in her appearance in Bognor, compared with the way she had looked in Bournemouth, Eastbourne, Weymouth and other seaside resorts. She had dark hair, which some people thought was a wig, and others said was not, and she made-up more – not exceptionally, just enough to be sure that passers-by were not likely to connect her with the woman whose photograph had been in all the newspapers for several days. It was now seldom seen, although the story of the investigation hit the headlines most days. Moreover, she had padded out her waist and her buttocks, and wore an elastic stocking on one leg, so that people noticed her leg and felt a little sorry because it was so swollen. She wore different clothes, too; dowdier.

Without studying her very closely, no one would have any reason to suspect that she was the wanted woman.

Twice a week, when the shops were crowded, she went to the nearest serve-yourself store and then on to the largest butcher's in town. The other trades-people called regularly. So she managed to buy everything needed at the bungalow while encountering very few people. Her cooking was good, and she fed Percy Whitehead well. Her one attempt to begin poisoning him, with arsenic, had proved that he was sensitive to the slightest stomach disorder. The weed-killer poison had been taken away with the rubbish, days ago.

She was more uneasy than she had been for some time. Her composure was good, but her nerves were raw. And Percy had behaved almost as if he was beginning to suspect that all was not well. She could not stay here much longer. Two days ago, she had found a small hoard of one-pound notes in an old suitcase, and she had taken that. When Percy was asleep this afternoon, she would search for other possible hiding places. The trouble with the blind was that they slept so lightly and their hearing was so acute.

On this, the fourth Wednesday in the month of May, the knowledge that she would soon have to leave Percy Whitehead gave her a kind of false contentment.

She had learned not to look away from policemen, to ignore people who stared at her, and to walk awkwardly, as befitted a woman with one bad leg.

Inside the bungalow, Percy Whitehead began a tour of investigation while Martha was out.

He kept that money in several different hiding places in the bungalow. He had a history of resentment at the loss of money in stocks and shares, a history of childhood insecurity, and in old age he had tended to keep plenty of ready money about him; he had, for years. It was in five different places, and he had known that it was quite secure before Martha had come, for he had gone and checked it all, with his perfect sureness of touch. This morning, he waited until the door had been closed for at least ten minutes, then began his quest. It was much colder than it had been, and Martha had told him that it was raining. She had gone out wrapped up in a mackintosh and carrying an umbrella.

The first cache was under a floorboard in this little dining-room, and the loose board was hidden by the carpet. He went down slowly on his knees, reached out for the corner of the carpet, felt that it was quite flat, and did not think that it had been rolled up lately, as it would have been if Martha had touched it. That reassured him. He rolled the carpet back, fingered the loose board, raised it slowly, and groped inside for the money which was wrapped in an old pillow case. The size of the bundle seemed normal, but to satisfy himself he unwrapped it, and counted each note; there were two hundred pounds, and his first count was exactly right.

"Perhaps I've misjudged her," he said hopefully.

He put everything back, and when the carpet was down again, trod on it to make sure that she would not notice that anyone had interfered with it. Then he went into the little front room, where the hiding place was exactly the same.

He found two hundred pounds there, also.

All this had taken him some time, but he knew that Martha was always out for at least an hour, and he had done the more difficult ones first; the other hiding places were quicker to get at. One was at the bottom of a mass of old papers in a suitcase; another was behind a loose brick in the chimney of his bedroom; the third was beneath a false top to his own wardrobe, one made before his sight had gone so badly. It was a matter only of minutes to check each of these, and his hearing was so acute that he would know as soon as Martha reached the garden gate. To make sure of this, he opened all of the front windows an inch or two; he could say that he had felt too warm. The radio had been playing softly, but he switched it off, so that it would not stop him from hearing Martha.

He wondered, as he touched the radio, why it was she always turned it off so that they did not hear the news.

He was more worried even than he admitted to himself about Martha.

The wardrobe money was there, the fireplace money, too; these he assessed by sense of touch, and did not count them; he could tomorrow. Finally he went to the suitcase, and unlocked it – and had his first shock when he felt a film of oily substance on the locks. His sensitive fingers picked that up in a moment.

He raised them to his nose and sniffed, and there was the unmistakable smell of machine oil, the kind that one would use for a sewing-machine. He wiped his fingers on his trousers carefully, then opened the lid of the case. All the loose papers were on top, but he was trembling as he delved for the money.

It wasn't there.

Two hundred pounds were missing.

He began to tremble, as from shock. He had half feared this, had been greatly relieved when the other hiding places had been found untouched, but this discovery affected him so much that his teeth chattered. He did not feel like closing the case and putting it away and pretending that he had noticed nothing, but he knew that it was what he ought to do. Then, next time he went out, he ought to go next door – he didn't know his neighbours but that didn't matter – and ask them to send for the police. Martha wasn't going to get away with this, the hypocritical old bitch.

He must lock the case again and push it under the bed.

He took his keys out of his pocket, and groped for the lock. Usually he would find it first go, but he was so upset and trembling so violently that the metal scraped on metal and he was like a drunken man trying to find the keyhole. He began to sweat as he listened for Martha; for some reason which he couldn't understand he was frightened.

He dropped the key.

He grabbed at it, to try to save it, and knocked the case off the bed. He heard it fall, heard the papers slithering and fluttering about, and knew that all the contents of the case were strewn about the room. It would take him an age to find and put them back, and he might not be able to make sure that he had them all. His whole body trembled as he stood the case upright and grabbed at some papers, but he had only put in two handfuls when he heard the garden gate open, and Martha walk towards the bungalow.

He stopped trying to hide what he had done.

He was a frail old man, and now he was very frightened.

All he could think of was getting out of the bungalow and going for help. He left everything just as it was, and turned towards the door, his sense of direction so good that he headed straight for it. He had his stick held out a little in front of him, and swung it more wildly than usual. He touched the open door, and reached the passage. He could hear Martha coming briskly along the garden path; she was always brisk when she approached the house. He turned towards the back door. He reached the kitchen, the door of which was open, and could smell the faint odour of the bacon which had been cooked this morning, and could smell something simmering; he could even hear it, although the gas beneath a stock-pot was turned so low that the soup hardly stirred at the top. The door to the back garden was almost adjacent to the gas stove, and was closed. He put out his stick, and heard the slight sound of metal on metal; his stick's ferrule on the enamel or iron of the stove. With agonising slowness, he slid the ferrule round so that he could judge the exact position of the stove, and therefore of the door. As he did so, an aeroplane overhead seemed to swoop low, making a hateful deafening sound. It roared and reverberated, but he dared not wait until it had gone before opening the door, he had to get out now.

He opened the door, and cool air swept into the kitchen.

"Why, Percy," said Martha, who was almost opposite him, "what on earth are you doing?"

She barred his path.

She had come sneaking round the back way.

He was a frail, frightened old man, although he could not really explain why he was so frightened. He only knew that he dared not stay in the bungalow alone with Martha.

"Percy!" Her voice was sharp.

"I'm going out," he muttered. "I've got every right to go out if I want to, I'm going out for a walk."

He stood squarely in the kitchen doorway, gripping his stick tightly; it was a foot off the ground. He could not see even the vague outline of Martha's body. He could not see the glitter in her eyes, or the way her lips tightened with a viciousness which few had ever seen.

She could see.

There he was, his lips parted, talking in short, gasping sentences, all the colour vanished from his cheeks, the stick held tightly in his hand and half raised, as if to strike her. She did not understand what had happened but was quite sure that this was a panic-stricken flight.

"Percy, don't be silly. Go back indoors. I'll take you out for a walk later." She kept her voice calm as she stretched out a small strong hand to take his wrists and to thrust him indoors. "I don't know what's come over you, to behave like this the moment my back's turned."

"Let me go!" gasped Percy Whitehead, and tried to free himself, but her grip was far too firm. "Let me go, you thieving hussy, let me go!"

Her grip tightened painfully and she twisted his wrists, meaning to hurt and to drive him inside. She glanced about nervously, but none of the neighbours seemed near. Percy's shout wasn't really very loud, his old voice was hoarse and didn't carry; high in the sky, an aeroplane droned.

"Let me go!"

"Get inside, or—"

She pushed him.

He staggered, and in staggering, freed himself from her grasp. Panic such as he had never known rose up in him. Her voice and the way she held and pushed him, told him that his fears were justified, and he dared not stay in the house with her. If only he could *see*. He raised his stick and struck at her, and she cried out. He shouted at the same time, and terror gave volume and pitch to his voice. He struck and struck, and shouted, too, felt her backing away, felt a moment of triumph and stepped swiftly after her.

He forgot the back door step, missed his footing, and fell.

With blood welling up from a scratch in her cheek, her wig awry, her knuckles grazed where the stick had struck her,

Martha Smallwood was still backing away from the old man when he fell. She felt a great, burning hatred for Whitehead because he had struck her, because he had tried to drive her from this sanctuary. He was there, helpless, with the stick on the ground. He tried to get up and stared at her piteously with those sightless eyes. She could pick up his own stick and beat the life out of him, she could—

She bent down for the stick.

She held her breath.

"Come on, get up and get inside," she said in a grating voice, "we'll settle this nonsense there." She bent down and took his arm and hauled him to his feet. He had never realised how strong she was.

The Sergeant in the charge room at the police station at Bognor lifted the telephone when it rang, and said: "Police Station," in a gruff but informal way.

"Is that the police station?" a woman asked.

"Yes, madam. Can I help you?"

"Well, I don't know, I don't want help myself, but—" The woman paused, while the Sergeant held on patiently, but began to make notes about another matter altogether; he felt pretty sure that this caller would simply waste his time. "I don't like spying on my neighbours," she began, only to pause again. The old so-and-so probably never kept her nose out of other people's business. "I don't know whether it's anything important, really, but I thought he was going to beat her brains out, I really did."

The Sergeant stopped writing.

"What's all this, madam? May I have your name and address, please?"

"My name's Carter, and I live at 28, Garden Road," she said, "and it's the blind man two doors away. I saw him attack his housekeeper. They had a terrible fight, and then he fell over. I saw her help him up, and now they're inside the bungalow, and I didn't know whether I ought to report it to the police or not.

He's such an old man. I've known him on and off for years, I can't think what could have made him so angry, but honestly, I thought—"

"We'll send someone along at once, madam," promised the Sergeant. "Mrs. Carter, of 28, Garden Road?"

"That's right."

"Where does the blind gentleman live?"

"Number 32."

"And when did this happen, Mrs. Carter?"

"Well, I don't really remember, I suppose it was getting on for an hour ago. I couldn't go out right away, not in my working clothes, and I couldn't make up my mind what to do, but it worried me so much I decided that I ought to report it."

"You were quite right, Mrs. Carter," said the Sergeant, "we'll send—"

"You won't tell anyone that I told you about it, will you?"

"We won't cause you any embarrassment at all, madam," promised the Sergeant. "Good-bye." He rang off, but did not immediately lift the telephone, for he could not make up his mind what to do. He could send a constable round, on his bicycle. He could wait until the Sergeant on the beat rang up, with his hourly report; he was due in ten minutes or so. Or he could tell the Super, who would probably send a car but might tear a strip off him for listening to an old woman's gossip.

A constable came in.

"Hallo, Jim," the Sergeant said, "you've got your bike today, haven't you? . . . That's good. Pop round to Number 32, Garden Road, and see if everything's okay there. Looks as if a blind chap who lives there was having a bit of a beano with his housekeeper."

The constable, a young man, said abruptly: "His housekeeper?"

He straddled his bicycle at once, and was outside the bungalow in Garden Road within ten minutes. As he walked up to the front door, he saw the curtains move, and believed that he saw a woman dodge out of sight. He strolled almost casually until he was close to the bungalow, then raced along the path at one side, towards the back. He saw a woman at the end of the garden, climbing a low fence which led to another garden, and a street beyond.

"Stop there!" the constable shouted, but the woman took no notice, dropped down to the other side, and began to run. The constable blew his whistle. The neighbour who had made the report appeared at her back doorsteps, several other people appeared. The constable vaulted the wall, landing as the running woman reached the shelter of a bungalow in the next street. His whistle shrilling, he tore after her.

Martha Smallwood was gasping for breath, her hair was loose, and she ran clumsily, but as if she believed she had a chance to get away. Then a dog came out of the house near her, yapping at her ankle. She shrieked and tried to dodge, but the dog nipped her, then squealed as she kicked it. It was her last effort, for the policeman grabbed her arm.

"Now what's all this about?" he demanded, and took a chance in a thousand. "Are you Martha *Smallwood?*"

"No, no, no!" Martha Smallwood screamed. "No, I'm not!"

"Let's go and see what's happened back there." The constable tightened his grip. "Come on." Then two other policemen arrived from a patrol car, and as they approached, Martha Smallwood fainted.

17

COINCIDENCE?

Gideon sat alone at his desk, later that same day, scanning the reports which had come in from the East End Divisions. They could hardly be better. Just as the death of Lee had caused panic among big-time thieves who had lost their main outlet for the goods they'd stolen, so the arrest of Ma Higgs spread dismay among the lesser fry. Hemmingway hadn't lost a moment. Once he had made sure that Ma was safely held, he had sent men round to all her credit customers. Some broke down almost at once, others were stubborn; but it was soon proved beyond doubt that Ma Higgs had been a big buyer, and that she in turn had handed the stolen goods over to women – perhaps one woman – in Petticoat Lane.

"And there's the go-between with Frisky Lee," Lemaitre declared. "Ten to one it's Tod's wife."

"Could be," said Gideon, as if sceptical. "Got that latest report from Warr ready yet?"

"Won't be half an hour." Lemaitre sat down hurriedly, and drew some papers closer. He avoided looking at Gideon for the next quarter of an hour, and the office was remarkably quiet, until a telephone bell rang. Lemaitre snatched off the receiver as if he wanted to break a record.

"Commander Gideon's office . . . Who? . . . All right, hold

on." He looked across, perkily. "Hemmy's on again, and sounds as if he's ready to jump as high as the roof."

"Thanks." Gideon lifted his extension of the same telephone. "What's on, Hemmy?"

"George, it never rains but it pours," said Hemmingway, and was as nearly excited as a senior policeman should ever be. "Two of Ma Higgs's customers say they've seen her take hot stuff into Tod Cowan's. That's the first time Tod's been named. He hasn't had a chance to move anything out of his shop since we've been watching him. How about picking him up, now?"

"Right away," agreed Gideon promptly. "You go along and see Tod in person, but forget to mention this job. He may feel that someone is going to squeal, but he can't be sure yet. Work on him about the Frisky Lee murder. Ask him to go into more detail about Ratsy Roden, and exactly what happened that morning. Let him think you're suspicious of him about that job. Work on him for half an hour, and then ask him to come along here for questioning. If he objects, fall back on the statements you've got, charge him, and bring him along."

"What's on your mind?" Hemmingway asked now, warily.

"I want to find out what he knows about Lee and Ratsy," Gideon said. "If we get him in the right frame of mind, he might come across. In the end he probably will, because he'll think it might help him to get off lightly."

"Cunning old so-and-so," said Hemmingway. "Okay. Wouldn't like Ma Higgs for the rest of the day, would you? I've got two policewomen looking after her, and they say she's the worst bitch they've ever had to handle. It took them an hour and a half to search her."

"Why don't you do the dirty work yourself?" Gideon grinned. "'Bye!" He rang off, and Lemaitre, who had listened to all this on his telephone, leaned back and pushed his hands through his thinning hair.

"So you've stopped being stubborn," he quipped.

"I know it's been said before," said Gideon, keeping a straight face, "but we really do get 'em all in the long run.

Then, unbidden, he had a mind picture of the boy Wray.

Early that evening two Detective-Sergeants and an Inspector were going through Ma Higgs's shop to see if they'd missed anything when the telephone bell rang at the back of the shop, and one of the Sergeants answered it.

"Corner Grocery Stores," he announced.

"Call from Birmingham for you, please hold on."

"Birmingham?" The Sergeant was surprised.

"Yes, sir, it's from a prepayment call-box."

"Sure it's—?"

"Quite sure, sir."

The Sergeant held on, wondering what Ma Higgs had to do with anyone in Birmingham, and wondering if this call would become useful later on. He held on for several seconds, until the operator said: "You're through," and a woman with a whiney kind of voice came on:

"Ma, is that you, dearie?"

"This is the Corner Grocery Stores," the Sergeant said, and tried to remember where he had heard that voice before.

Peter Wray's mother stood in the kiosk at Birmingham Central Station, where she had made the call because she knew it would be difficult to trace. She was waiting anxiously for Ma Higgs to speak, and had one of the big shocks of her life at the sound of a man's voice. She sensed the truth in a flash. The voice was deep and had a kind of ring of authority about it, not like that of any of Ma's men friends, or men customers.

Mrs. Wray said : "Where—where's Mrs. Higgs?"

"Mrs. Higgs isn't here at the moment, can I help you?"

"I—I dunno," said Jane Wray, and then went all to pieces. There was danger wherever there was a policeman, and it was all too possible that she would be recognised. "No, it's okay," she said hurriedly. "I wanted a talk with Ma, it's all right, okay."

She rang off.

She went out of the box, wiping her forehead, looking hot and harassed, as if with bad news. She walked slowly away from the telephone box towards the exit, and as she neared the streets, she muttered to herself:

"They've got her all right, she had it coming."

Then: "Someone's bound to find the kid. Bound to."

Peter was in a kind of sleep, aware of where he was, aware of wanting the door to open, and yet not longing for it, as he usually did. Near his hand as he lay on his side, was the sticky bag in which the sweets had been.

None of the sweets were left.

For the first time since the police had been to the flat, Reginald Dennis felt free to breathe. He had expected a lot of awkwardness and some tricky questions, but hadn't expected the police inquiry to take so long. Now he sensed from the manner of the Superintendent in charge, the man Sparrow, that the police had almost given up hope: not suspicion, but hope.

Sparrow asked a few questions which meant little, and then left the flat.

He was frowning as he walked to his car.

"I'll have to tell Gee-Gee that I can't find a thing to pin on to Dennis," he said gloomily. "It wouldn't matter if I wasn't so sure that the young swine pushed her out of the window."

The best way, Robert Carne decided, was to stage a car accident. If he knew anything about any single subject, it was about cars. He knew exactly what made them tick, and what made them stick, and he knew just what kind of little mechanical trouble could cause disaster at the right place and the right time. Marion had a driving licence, and had passed her test several years ago, but she had told him that she hadn't driven a car for over a year. He had told her how useful it would be if she took up driving again, it would help her to make local deliveries of the accessories, and would take a lot of work off his shoulders, and make sure that he was home more often. She had been delighted. He had taken her out in his car, twice, and judged the quality of her driving. She shouldn't really be let loose on the road, she was one of those to whom driving would always be something of a mystery. No road sense. No judgment. His was an old car with a gear shift, and she even had some difficulty in changing gear, especially if there was the slightest threat of emergency.

He could rig the steering column, or the brakes.

He had to decide what hill she should drive down, and the details of the "accident". The best thing would be for him to telephone her from somewhere on the outskirts of London, and ask her to come and fetch him. She wouldn't like to say no. All he had to make sure was that she would have to go down a hill. He accepted the fact that she might not be killed, but with luck she would be. If she was simply injured, or maimed, then he wouldn't have to worry about her for a long time, and he would make do with the money he'd got for the "business". He hadn't spent much of it yet, and directly the accident was reported, he could change his mind, saying that he would have to wait until his wife recovered.

That evening, he took her out in the car, and told her to drive. She crashed her gears and hit the kerb, then drove for ten minutes without incident, although she had a tendency to pull in towards the kerb whenever she saw another car approaching.

"You're doing fine," Carne assured her, squeezing her arm. "Don't worry about being jumpy, precious, you'll soon get over that. All you need is practice. You want to get out in the car a bit more on your own."

"Darling, I feel so useless."

"I know – and it's just lack of confidence, I tell you."

"I wish I could agree."

"Listen, Marion," said Carne more firmly, "it will save us ten or twelve pounds a week if you can drive the car, and you're as capable as the next one. Don't throw the chance away because you haven't the courage to go out on your own. Take every chance you can of driving, and in a week or two you'll forget that you were ever nervous."

"All right, darling," Marion said, in a subdued voice.

Carne was quite sure that he had got her into the right mood. He had used the words "haven't the courage" deliberately, and although she hadn't said so, they had hurt. When he decided on the night of the accident and telephoned for her, she would take the car out if it killed her.

He grinned.

If it killed her was right!

Arkwright would have dropped his inquiries following the chance encounter with Roger Clayton, in spite of the time he had spent on investigating, but for the sudden tightening up at the Yard. He was keenly aware of a chance of early promotion if he could pull off a neat job, and believed that he had Gideon's goodwill. So he went over everything he had done, including his visit to the Cork Street Registry Office, and decided to go there again. He studied the register closely, and found the Robert Carne-Marion Lane certificate. The initials were almost certainly coincidence. He checked, and found that three other men had been married during the past two weeks, each with the initials R. C. So that didn't mean a thing. But this Robert Carne had been married on the day that he, Arkwright, had seen Roger Clayton all spruced up and wearing a carnation in his button-hole.

Arkwright went to see the registrar, an elderly man, who might protest that he married hundreds of couples, and couldn't expect to remember them all. Arkwright had a photograph of Roger Clayton with him, and showed it.

"Have you ever seen this man, Mr. Green?"

"Oh, yes," answered Green. "I married him only about three weeks ago. There were two witnesses, both on the bride's side. Let me see." He went to his precious books and began to check, while Arkwright felt a quickening excitement, and at the same time a sense of guilt. He should have brought that photograph in before, had actually thought of doing so; but this wasn't strictly speaking "a case" and he hadn't troubled.

"This is the address from which he was married, and this is the address she gave," reported the registrar. "I can't be sure they are living at either of the addresses now. I do hope there is nothing serious, Sergeant."

"Just routine," Arkwright said, and went first to the house where Marion Lane had lived on her own, after turning it into two flats. It was there that he learned that she had let the flat to an old friend who had been a witness at the wedding ceremony: a Miss Ethel Jones. But Ethel Jones wasn't in during the day.

Arkwright decided to go back to see her that night; she might know where the Carnes *alias* the Claytons had gone to live.

It did not then occur to Arkwright that there might be any desperate hurry, and he went back to the Yard and began to inquire,' at routine speed, into the history of Marion Carne, *née* Lane.

It didn't take him long to discover that she had inherited a small fortune; then Arkwright really felt the need for haste.

Arkwright was on his way to see Ethel Jones, Marion was driving the car round the block, for practice after dark, the child Peter lay in a coma on the floor of the cupboard, Ma Higgs still stormed at her captors, Tod Cowan had admitted nothing and was on his way with Hemmingway to the Yard, where Gideon was waiting for him, and Jane Wray was in a back street pub, drinking gin and water.

A little before eight o'clock, Gideon had finished all the office work he wanted to do. He did not feel really relaxed, and still condemned himself for slackness and for allowing others to be slack. When the telephone bell rang he thought it was to announce Hemmingway and his prisoner.

"Will you speak to Superintendent Warr, sir, from Bognor?"

There was another job to nag at him.

"Yes, put him on." There was a pause, and then Warr spoke.

"Gideon speaking," Gideon said. "How are things going?"

Warr said: "We've got Martha Smallwood, George. Got her early this afternoon, but I didn't worry you then, I wanted to be absolutely sure, and to get the story straight."

The bloody fool, thought Gideon, to keep this to himself! But Warr was going on, obviously relieved and satisfied.

"She was housekeeper to a blind man, seems to have robbed him already. He cottoned on to what she was up to and ran into trouble, but he's all right now – in hospital, suffering from shock, but nothing serious. As a matter of fact," went on Warr reluctantly, "no one can really claim any credit. A neighbour happened to see . . .

"But at least the rest of it is sewn up," Warr finished, confidently. "I've got all the evidence the Public Prosecutor could want for half a dozen murder prosecutions. I'll need a couple of days down here, then I'll be ready."

"Fine," said Gideon. "Take an extra day if you need it."

He rang off, muttered: "Fool," picked up his pipe, and was filling it when he heard a man coming briskly along the passage. The footsteps stopped outside, there was a tap, and on Gideon's "Come in" Hemmingway entered.

"Hallo, George!" His lined face was bright with deep satisfaction. "I've got Tod Cowan downstairs in the waiting-room. Brought him along myself."

"He said anything?"

"Not yet," said Hemmingway, "but I think he'll soon crack."

18

TOD COWAN

Gideon walked downstairs to the waiting-room with Hemmingway, and as he neared the room he saw Detective-Sergeant Arkwright, his expression clearly one of excitement, hurrying towards the lift. Just coming in, too, were two hefty Flying Squad men with a little chap sandwiched between them. The little chap was Hungry Dory, who looked as if he would collapse if touched, but was the quickest and most able cat burglar then operating.

Gideon paused.

"Half a minute," he said to Hemmingway, and saw Hungry Dory looking at him with pretended pathos, his huge eyes and hollow cheeks wrongly suggesting that he was on the verge of starvation. "Why don't you keep out of trouble, Hungry?"

"It's me wife," said Hungry, in a whining voice. "Don't ever make the mistake I did if your wife dies on you, Gee-Gee. Married a girl young enough to be my daughter, I did, you can guess why, and I'm not saying I've got any complaints in that direction, but talk about greedy! Proper voracious, that's what she is. Silver fox and Persian lamb are beneath her, she'll only settle for mink. And when I come to thinking of all the old hags in London dripping with mink, and my Susie all ready to win a beauty competition I couldn't resist it, Gee-Gee, that's Gawd's truth."

It probably was, too.

"Where'd you pick him up?" Gideon asked the Squad men.

"Climbing in a house in Wyman Square."

"All right, take him in to Mr. Squires, he might be able to knock some sense into him."

"If only I'd had the sense to stay a widower, that was my big mistake," Hungry said, and flicked his hand in salute to Gideon as they took him off. Hemmingway stood by impatiently, but Arkwright was still hovering.

"Want me, Sergeant ?" asked Gideon.

"If you could spare a minute, sir."

"Half an hour's time do? I'll be more free then."

"Any time to suit you, sir."

"Wait down in the canteen. I'll call you," Gideon said, and went to the waiting-room with Hemmingway. Arkwright walked towards the stairs and the canteen, to wait.

Robert Carne was in a pub, at the top of Putney Hill. The steepness of the hill was exactly right, if he could only think of a way of getting Marion up to the top, ready to drive down. He knew she would put all her weight on the brakes when she started the descent, she wouldn't think of changing gear, and the fast-running car would scare her. The brakes were fixed so that they couldn't stand any sudden pressure.

Putney Hill was perfect.

If he told her to drive to Wimbledon first, and if he wasn't at a rendezvous there, to come and pick him up by the traffic lights at Putney Bridge, it ought to be all right, unless she came the long way round, to avoid the hill. If he told her Roehampton, say out by the Star and Garter

Home, it would be safer.

The little tailor with the jaunty manner, standing outside his shop door and rubbing his hands on a crowded Sunday morning, was hardly recognisable. Gideon looked at him intently, and wondered whether he was frightened only of the police and what they could do. Tod looked shabby, too; it was an old trick to make oneself seem poor and hard-done-by. Here was the man who had been a collector for Lee, who probably knew most of Lee's secrets; who might and probably did know who had killed Lee.

Hemmingway was by Gideon's side, a Sergeant from the Division and a Yard constable were by Tod's. Tod licked his lips, and closed his heavily-lidded eyes as if he would faint.

Gideon said: "Well, you're in for a stretch, you bloody fool."

"Mr. Gideon," began Tod, and couldn't go on. He swallowed hard, and tried again. "Mr. Gideon, you've no right to say a thing like that. I can't understand it, I always thought you were a fair-minded policeman, and now I find you're as bad as the rest of them. I'm disappointed, I . . ." He couldn't finish, and his lips were quivering as the words faded away.

"All I want and all any policeman wants is a clean East End," Gideon said, "and we thought you were one of the people we could rely on. You've let us down so hard that you deserve twenty years."

"But I haven't!"

"Don't be a fool," Gideon said. Tod Cowan didn't yet know about the witnesses against him, he was ostensibly here because of the investigations into Frisky Lee's death. "Let's have the truth now. What did you say to Ratsy to make him leave your shop that Sunday morning? He came to you for help and you drove him out."

"I swear I didn't, Mr. Gideon!"

Gideon kept silent for a few seconds, staring down, and guessing at the anguish in Cowan's mind. No one moved or spoke, but now Cowan began to rub his hands together, with a sliding noise; and his mouth worked more.

Gideon said: "We picked up Ma Higgs today. We've picked up a lot of other people who've been in the game. We know you were in with Frisky Lee. What happened, Cowan? Did he press you too hard? Did you kill him?"

Cowan really swayed, and would probably have fallen but for the policeman's quick grab. What little colour he had faded, even his lips seemed to be colourless. Gideon stood over him like an avenging angel.

"I didn't kill him, Mr. Gideon, I swear I didn't. A long time ago I committed a serious crime, and Lee knew about it: he said he would shop me if I didn't do what he wanted. How could I help myself, Mr. Gideon? I didn't want to lose everything I'd got, did I? I tried to stand aside, I swear I did, but Lee sent a couple of his bruisers round to see me, they— well, Mr. Hemmingway will remember what happened," Cowan went on, in the same helpless voice. "I had an accident, said I'd fallen down the stairs, but Lee's men beat me up. I was three months a cripple, Mr. Gideon, and just couldn't stand out any longer. That's the truth. Lee made me agree to act as his agent. I never kept the stuff long, always got rid of it quick, Lee had a dozen outlets, see. I did the work and took the risks, while he—"

"Did you kill him, Cowan?"

"No! Ratsy did, I've told you!"

"What made Ratsy leave your shop?"

Cowan hesitated, hands rubbing together almost fiercely. Gideon didn't prompt him; just waited. And the answer came at last, the answer to a question which might never have been asked.

"I—I had to send him out, he—"

"After Lee was dead?"

"Yes, I—"

"You weren't scared of Lee when he was dead."

"No, I can't explain, I just can't."

"Who made you do it, Cowan? What made you drive Ratsy out? Come on, tell me."

Sweat was trickling down Cowan's face, and Gideon felt sure that he would soon crack, provided the pressure was not eased.

"Let's have the truth now. No one made you, you killed Lee

yourself, and then you framed Ratsy."

"Mr. Gideon, it's not true!"

"Superintendent, take careful note of what I'm going to say," Gideon said to Hemmingway formally. "Cowan, I'm going to charge you with the murder of Harold James known as Frisky Lee at his home in Medd Alley at or about six o'clock in the morning of . . ."

"No!" Cowan gasped, and Gideon had never seen a more piteous sight. "It was Ratsy who killed him, but they drove him to it! They told Ratsy Lee was going to throw him over, they drove Ratsy almost mad. They drove him—"

"Who drove him?" roared Gideon.

"God forgive me," Cowan whispered hoarsely, "it was the women. Ada's mother and"—he almost choked—"and my wife. They—they both worked with Lee for years, my—my own wife did, even before me. It was Ada's mother who fixed Lee's marriage. Then Lee said he was going to clear out to Australia and leave them all flat. They drove Ratsy to kill him, then *made* me cover up. I had to do it, Gideon, my own wife was involved. What else could a man do?"

So his fat chunk of a wife with her dyed hair *had* squashed him. And Ada Lee's mother had fooled Gideon and the others with those bold flashing eyes, and her fierce "protectiveness" towards her daughter.

Poor Ada?

"Yes, I knew they'd driven Ratsy to do it," Ada Lee admitted helplessly, "but I daren't say anything. They—they said if I did they'd take my baby away. They said they'd take my baby."

"Hallo, George," Lemaitre greeted, when they got back to Gideon's office. "'Lo, Hemmy. George, an old pal of yours wants to talk to you. Says he's acting for Ma Higgs, and two poor, misunderstood, ill-treated sweet little women. Name of Gabriel Lyon. He says he'd like to talk to you personally."

Gideon looked thoughtfully into Lemaitre's eyes, and then

said: "We'll let him call again."

"He'd defend the swine who killed his own mother," Hemmingway said disgustedly.

"I dunno," said Gideon, and for some inexplicable reason, he felt flat. "It'll be interesting to see which way he tries to jump. Lem, ring the canteen and have them send Sergeant Arkwright up, will you? Hemmy, anything else tonight?"

"All okay by me, George. Wouldn't like to come across for a quick one, would you?"

"Not tonight, thanks," said Gideon, and leaned back in his chair and picked up a receiver. He said to the operator: "Get my wife, will you? I'll hold on." He smoothed the bowl of his pipe with his free hand, while Lemaitre talked to the canteen, and Hemmingway looked steadily at him, as if trying to see what went on inside the mind of George Gideon. "Hallo—hallo, Kate . . . I'm fine . . . Eh . . . No, I shouldn't wait up, that's what I called about. Several things to do, and I'm sure to be late. Just thought I'd save you wearing the armchair out . . . No, don't leave anything, I'll have something to eat before I leave here . . ." Gideon grinned. "Yes, I promise! . . . 'Bye, dear." He rang off, and for a moment looked almost as if all anxieties had been lifted off his shoulder, but that was not for long.

Lemaitre said: "Arkwright's on his way."

"Anything else in?"

"Only the usual. Couple of beatings up, nasty job out at Camberwell, two men broke into a doctor's place, and knocked him about badly. They . . ."

"The Division checking for any stolen drugs?"

"I'll make sure," said Lemaitre, and jotted down a note. "Then there was a girl on Clapham Common, couple of swine attacked her. Cashier at the Roxy, Ealham Cross, robbed of the night's takings, about three hundred quid. Must have a good show on there. Night's only just started, of course."

Gideon said: "Yes," and then Hemmingway went out, rather subdued, and Gideon wondered whether he should have gone across with the NE man for that drink, after all.

Footsteps sounded in the passage.

"Come in," Lemaitre called, after a tap, and the door opened and Arkwright stepped inside, closing the door quickly but quietly, looking big and well-groomed, and showing signs of repressed impatience. He drew himself up to attention. Gideon let him stay like that; he would learn soon enough that it wasn't necessary. For Arkwright, this was a big occasion, there was no need to spoil it.

"The Carne job?" Gideon asked.

"Yes, sir. I've made one or two discoveries today that might help." Gideon heard of the coincidence of the R. C. initials, and the registrar's quick recognition of the photograph, and then Arkwright went on: "So tonight I went to the place where the new wife used to live, sir. A friend lives there now. Carne decided to live somewhere else in London, and the two girls haven't met since. The friend isn't sure they're back from the honeymoon – she doesn't know where they spent it, but Marion Lane, as she was, wrote to her, postmark Brighton, and said she and her new husband are going into business in a big way. She didn't say that she was putting up the money, but hinted at it. She said they're getting some showrooms in Kensington High Street. Car accessory salerooms. It's all remarkably like the original job when Clayton, as Carne was then, lost his wife. She had money, they started a joint business, and . . ."

Gideon let him finish, and then asked: "What else have you done?"

"Well, sir, I've found out where they're living." This was Arkwright's reason for elation: he was really a fast worker. "Mrs. Carne said they were likely to take a service apartment, so I telephoned round to about fifty places, and finally got the one they're at. Byng Court, Chelsea."

Gideon handed out the proper meed of praise. "Quick work, Arkwright, thanks. Now, we've got to be careful, but we still have to work fast. If he's planning to do away with his wife, he may fix it soon. I think we'd better have him questioned."

Lemaitre broke in: "What for? Getting married?"

"Using an assumed name," said Gideon. "We can tell him we want to make sure he isn't a bigamist. Get him on his own, though. We don't want complications with his wife." Gideon hesitated, knowing that he could detail Arkwright to his job, and give the Sergeant a chance he had been waiting for for a long time. But a more experienced man might do it better, this job was fraught with complications. Arkwright tried to look as if it didn't matter, and that influenced Gideon to give him his chance. "Try and see Carne tonight, Sergeant, and if you can't, get at him early in the morning. Question him closely about the change of name, and let me know his reaction."

"Yes, sir."

Arkwright could not hide his smile of satisfaction as he went out.

"If Carne is on the up and up, and Arkwright makes a mess of it and lets the wife know . . ." Lemaitre began.

"He won't," said Gideon, with a bluff confidence. "He'll make sure he doesn't put a foot wrong. Oh, damn the telephone." He picked up the receiver at once. "Gideon," he greeted, and listened. Then, "Good evening, Mr. Lyon, I'm sorry I didn't ring you, I've been rushing round all the evening."

"I can well believe it," said Gabriel Lyon, in his gentle voice. "I have been fairly active myself. Mr. Gideon, will you forgive me if I ask a question which you might regard as impertinent?"

"I don't have to answer," Gideon said.

"I know that only too well," said Lyon, but he didn't give the hint of a laugh which might have suggested he was in good humour. "Are the Cowans and Ada Lee's mother under arrest?"

"Yes."

"On what charges?"

Gideon said: "Are you acting for them?"

"Until I know the charges, I cannot decide."

Gideon explained briskly, and after a short pause Lyon said very quietly: "So they were deeply involved in the training of children, as well as other matters."

"Yes."

"I shall not act for them," Lyon said, "but I shall continue to act for young Ada Lee. Have you accounted for all the children involved?"

"We've found all of the mothers and children involved except a Mrs. Wray and her son Peter. If you can help us to find out where they are, it'll be a load off my mind."

"Anything I can find out I'll pass on," Lyon promised.

Peter was breathing, but he hadn't moved for some time. The dark cupboard had that sickly smell.

"Listen, darling, you've got to take a hold on yourself," said Carne into the telephone. "You can drive as well as anyone. Meet me at the Green Man, top of Putney Hill. If I'm not there, I'll be at the station, in the High Street."

"Bob, I hate . . ." Marion began, but checked herself, because she didn't want him to despise her.

She had been going to say that she hated driving down steep hills.

Bob wasn't at the Green Man, and she started the car again, and headed for the top of the steep hill which led to Putney High Street.

The headlights of cars coming up the hill seemed to make it even steeper than it was, and she clenched her teeth.

"Don't be a fool," she breathed. Holding the wheel very tightly and moving into third gear, she went over the brow. On her side, the road ahead was clear. Her foot touched the brake all the time, she was so determined not to go too fast. The car gathered speed, in spite of the low gear, and she was not expert enough to change down further; she was genuinely frightened, and still clenching her teeth.

She put her foot on the brake, and felt something odd; a lack of resistance. The car didn't slacken speed. She tried again and nothing happened; and she screamed:

"Bob, Bob, Bob!"

She felt the steering wheel swinging in her hand and turned towards the kerb, which seemed to rush at her.

19

SEARCH

Gideon opened the front door of his house just after midnight. The small landing light was on, but all the rooms were in darkness, and were quiet. He closed the door quietly and then put on the hall light and walked along to the kitchen. For the first time since Woodrow had reported, he smiled; not broadly, but with a smile which would have done his wife good had she known how it had to be forced out of him. For on the kitchen table was an upturned pudding basin, keeping sandwiches fresh, and by the side was a tea-tray with everything ready, all he had to do was boil the kettle. Standing by all this was a bottle of beer.

He made tea, ate sandwiches, and went upstairs at half-past twelve. He stepped heavily, for his spirits were low. He could not prevent himself from accepting part of the blame for the fact that the Wray boy couldn't be traced.

He went into the bedroom cautiously. Long since, he had put in a low-wattage lamp, just enough for him to see by when he got in late; light rather than movement disturbed Kate. There she lay, sleeping, the clothes drawn right up to her chin, a hair-net keeping her thick, wavy hair in place. As he undressed, she stirred, and said in a vague and sleepy voice: "Hallo, dear."

"You don't want to wake up, Kate."

"G'night."

She was breathing evenly again when Gideon got into bed. He thought that he was tired, but soon began to realise that he wasn't going to get off to sleep. He kept picturing the woman striking the child, at Hyde Park Corner. Good God, that was a month ago! And then, pale and subdued – cowed – in Petticoat Lane, a week later.

It was warm, and soon Gideon felt too hot. He turned, cautiously, but couldn't lie on his other side for long. He was wider awake than he had been before, moving a leg, an arm, shifting his great body, his head, even his hands. It was no use, he would have to get up and go downstairs and try to read. He pushed the bedclothes back, and as he did so, Kate asked in a wide-awake voice: "Can't you sleep?"

"No."

"Why not, dear?"

"Oh, this and that," he answered.

She stretched out and put on a bedside lamp, then hitched herself up a little on her pillows. For once, her hair-net kept in the right position. The deep V of her nightdress showed the full, curving beauty of her breast. She drew the sides of the V together, without thinking, and as Gideon also sat up, she said: "Did you have supper?"

"Oh, yes, thanks. Jolly good."

"What's on your mind, George?"

He told her, quietly, slowly, deliberately. In fact he was thinking aloud. There were the things left undone because he hadn't been thorough enough, and the things left undone by others – to whom he had given a lead. In a way, he was pleading with himself: that he should dedicate himself more so as to make these errors of omission impossible. He did not put this into plain words, but obviously it was on his mind. He looked up at the ceiling, across at the window, at the mirror where Kate was reflected but he was not, so far as he could see. He seldom looked at Kate herself, but they sat there together, his arm round her shoulders, his hand at her breast, almost impersonally.

". . . the hell of it is, these kids," he said. "I'm not thinking of this Peter Wray, except as an example of what's happening. What kind of lives do they lead? What gets into the mind of a mother to do it to her child? And how many are there like it still? We've caught one group, that's all. Hundreds upon hundreds, in one way or other, even those who aren't being trained in crime, are being allowed to run around loose, the National Society for Prevention of Cruelty to Children deals with tens of thousands of cases a year. Until we can stop it, we're going to have generation after generation of criminals, and we simply can't stop it. Or we don't seem able to."

Kate said quietly: "It's hardly your job, George."

"Oh, no," he said bitterly. "It's not our job until they're criminals. Even if we're lucky enough to catch 'em when they're really young, they've had the training and they've been taught to think the police are a lot of brutes and bullies and the law a thing to laugh at. They're sent to a home, or later to Borstal, and if you think every child who goes to a home or Borstal comes out cured, you're wrong. Kate, I've been thinking about the kids I know. The kids in families where the mother and father are always in and out of jail, who run around in little gangs, and—"

He broke off.

All he was saying seemed futile. This eruption of thoughts which had simmered beneath the surface of his mind might ease the pressure a little, but that was all.

Kate couldn't do anything, except listen; but she did listen, and he believed that she understood.

She put her hand on his; there was nothing impersonal about the way she did that.

"Darling, you must get some sleep," she said. "The first day you have off, we'll talk about it again, not just snatch at it like this." So she hoped to quieten his restlessness, and perhaps that would. "Couldn't you make some arrangement to have all the men on the beats make a note of the children who seem worst off? I know it can't be done officially, but I should think most of the men would help, and most of the Divisions, too. Once you really know how many bad cases there are, you might be able to do something with the N.S.P.C.C."

That wasn't soothing syrup.

His eyes were suddenly brighter. "That's an idea," he agreed, "we might be able to make something of it. Bless you, Kate."

He slid his arms round her, and drew her close.

Afterwards, he slept, completely at peace.

There was no message at the house when he left at half-past eight; a bad sign, he decided. He drove faster than usual towards the Yard. The men on duty outside and the other C.I.D. men on their way or coming away from the offices were on the look-out anyhow, for Gideon's mood had been enough to alert everyone. He slammed the door of his car and walked with springy strides towards the steps, hurried up them, greeted the Sergeant and the constable on duty in the hall, and found himself with two Superintendents going up in the lift.

"Don't know what you've been doing to Arkwright," one of them said.

"Sergeant Arkwright?"

"You know damned well it's Sergeant Arkwright. He's twice the man he was. Hear about last night?"

"What?"

"He spent the whole evening trying to find out more about this chap Carne or Clayton, and about eleven o'clock found out that Carne's wife had met with an accident. She wasn't badly hurt, though. Brakes failed on Putney Hill, but she'd changed down to low gear and had the sense to turn into the kerb. The moment he heard about it, Arkwright decided to have that car checked, and spent part of the night doing it himself. He thinks the brakes might have been tampered with, but can't be sure yet."

"Keep him on the job," urged Gideon.

"Oh, I shall."

The lift stopped. Gideon hurried along to his own office. The door was ajar, as always, and when he went in there was Lemaitre and an elderly Sergeant, putting the finishing touches to the report of the night's crimes. Gideon slapped his hat on a peg, and said breezily: "'Morning, you two. Anything about that Wray kid?"

"Haven't even found out where the mother lives," answered Lemaitre. "Don't know what you're so steamed up about, George, she might be hiding out wherever she lives, might even have taken the kid out of town until things cool down a bit." Lemaitre turned to the reports, of all and sundry crimes.

A telephone bell rang. Lemaitre lifted his receiver, and then looked up at Gideon and said: "Hemmy wants you." Gideon plucked his instrument up, and said almost sharply: "Gideon. Yes, Hemmy, I—"

Lemaitre and the Sergeant saw the way his expression changed, saw the bleakness fade, saw his smile grow, and realised how real a human being he was. He sat on the corner of his desk, one foot touching the floor, listening and nodding as if Hemmingway could see him, and finally saying: "That's fine. Wonderful. You really are going out in a blaze of glory! Yes, I'll be over."

He rang off.

He looked across at Lemaitre.

"They found the Wray kid," he reported. "The bitch had locked him in a cupboard in the back room where they lived. Hemmingway had asked that copper, Smith, to be seconded to him, as Smith knew the woman pretty well. Smith's description did the trick, they soon found the room. Kid must have been there for twenty-four hours. He was in a stupor, but is coming through all right."

"Another one in the bag," Lemaitre said, with deep satisfaction, and grinned. "We certainly do get 'em in the end, don't we, George? Well, I can't say I'm sorry tomorrow's Sunday, it's been quite a week."

JOHN CREASEY

GIDEON'S DAY

Gideon's day is a busy one. He balances family commitments with solving a series of seemingly unrelated crimes from which a plot nonetheless evolves and a mystery is solved.

One of the most senior officers within Scotland Yard, George Gideon's crime solving abilities are in the finest traditions of London's world famous police headquarters. His analytical brain and sense of fairness is respected by colleagues and villains alike.

'The finest of all Scotland Yard series' – *New York Times.*

GIDEON'S FIRE

Commander George Gideon of Scotland Yard has to deal successively with news of a mass murderer, a depraved maniac, and the deaths of a family in an arson attack on an old building south of the river. This leaves little time for the crisis developing at home ....

'Gideon of Scotland Yard emerges as one of the most real working detectives in modern fiction.... A sympathetic and believable professional policeman.' - *New York Times*

JOHN CREASEY

THE CREEPERS

"The prisoner's hand was thin and bony ... And in the centre of the palm was a pinkish mark. It was the shape of a wolf's head, mouth open, fangs showing. Although it was what he had expected to see, Inspector West felt a twinge of repugnance a stab not unrelated to fear. It was the fifth time he had seen the mark of the wolf – the mark of Lobo."

A gang of cat burglars led by Lobo cause mayhem as they terrorize the city. They must be stopped, but with little in the way of evidence the police are baffled. Just how can Inspector West manage to do this in what is a race against time before more victims succumb?

"Here is an excellent novel of law enforcement officers, harried, discouraged and desperately fatigued, moving inexorably ahead under the pressure of knowledge that they must succeed to save human lives." - Cleveland Plain-Dealer

"Furiously exciting" - Chicago Tribune

"The action is fast, continuous and exciting" - San Francisco News

John Creasey

The House of the Bears

Standing alone in the bleak Yorkshire Moors is Sir Rufus Marne's 'House of the Bears'. Dr. Palfrey is asked to journey there to examine an invalid - who has now disappeared. Moreover, Marne's daughter lies terribly injured after a fall from the minstrel's gallery which Dr. Palfrey discovers was no accident. He sets out to investigate and the results surprise even him . . . .

"'Palfrey' and his boys deserve to take their places among the immortals." - Western Mail

Introducing the Toff

Whilst returning home from a cricket match at his father's country home, the Honourable Richard Rollison - alias The Toff - comes across an accident which proves to be a mystery. As he delves deeper into the matter with his usual perseverance and thoroughness , murder and suspense form the backdrop to a fast moving and exciting adventure.

'The Toff has been promoted to a place of honour among amateur detectives.' – The Times Literary Supplement

Printed in Great Britain
by Amazon